GREAT STORIES IN EASY ENGLISH

# TREASURE ISLAND

R.L. Stevenson

Abridged and Simplified by

**S.E. PACES**

S. CHAND
AN ISO 9001:2000 COMPANY

# S. CHAND & COMPANY LTD.

7361, Ram Nagar, New Delhi-110 055

# S. CHAND & COMPANY LTD.

**(An ISO 9001:2000 Company)**

*Head Office* : 7361, RAM NAGAR, NEW DELHI - 110 055
Phones : 23672080-81-82; Fax : 91-11-23677446
Shop at : **schandgroup.com**
E-mail : **schand@vsnl.com**

*Branches* :

- 1st Floor, Heritage, Near Gujarat Vidhyapeeth, Ashram Road,
  **Ahmedabad**-380 014. Ph : 7541965, 7542369
- No. 6, Ahuja Chambers, 1st Cross, Kumara Krupa Road,
  **Bangalore**-560 001. Ph : 2268048, 2354008
- 152, Anna Salai, **Chennai**-600 002. Ph : 28460026
- S.C.O. 6, 7 & 8, Sector 9D, **Chandigarh**-160017, Ph : 2749376, 2749377
- 1st Floor, Bhartia Tower, Badambadi, **Cuttack**-753 009, Ph : 2332580; 2332581
- 1st Floor, 52-A, Rajpur Road, **Dehradun**-248 011. Ph : 2740889, 2740861
- Pan Bazar, **Guwahati**-781 001. Ph : 2522155
- Sultan Bazar, **Hyderabad**-500 195. Ph : 24651135, 24744815
- Mai Hiran Gate, **Jalandhar** - 144008. Ph : 2401630
- 613-7, M.G. Road, Ernakulam, **Kochi**-682 035. Ph : 2381740
- 285/J, Bipin Bihari Ganguli Street, **Kolkata**-700 012. Ph : 22367459, 22373914
- Mahabeer Market, 25 Gwynne Road, Aminabad, **Lucknow**-226 018. Ph : 2226801, 2284815
- Blackie House, 103/5, Walchand Hirachand Marg , Opp. G.P.O., **Mumbai**-400 001.
  Ph : 22690881, 22610885
- 3, Gandhi Sagar East, **Nagpur**-440 002. Ph : 2723901
- 104, Citicentre Ashok, Govind Mitra Road, **Patna**-800 004. Ph : 2671366, 2302100

*Marketing Offices :*
- 238-A M.P. Nagar, Zone 1, **Bhopal**-462 011
- A-14 Janta Store Shopping Complex, University Marg, Bapu Nagar, **Jaipur**-302 015,
  Phone : 0141-2709153

ISBN : 81-219-2412-X

*Illustrations re-illustrated by :*
Anil Parganiha & Harish Parganiha

PRINTED IN INDIA

*By Rajendra Ravindra Printers (Pvt.) Ltd., 7361, Ram Nagar, New Delhi-110 055 and published by S. Chand & Company Ltd., 7361, Ram Nagar, New Delhi-110 055.*

# CONTENTS

# INTRODUCTION

ROBERT LOUIS STEVENSON (1850-1894) is famous for his stories of adventure. He was born in Scotland. Poor health led him to travel to sunnier lands and he died in the tropical island of Samoa.

"Treasure Island" is his best adventure story. Boys and girls all over the world have been delighted by this book. It is full of excitement. Jim Hawkins, a Scottish boy, finds a map of an island showing where a pirate's treasure is hidden. With the village doctor and the squire, he sails over the seas to look for it. A band of pirates, led by Long John Silver, are also after the treasure. After many exciting adventures, Jim and his friends find the treasure and sail safely home.

# THE CAPTAIN COMES TO THE ADMIRAL BENBOW INN

Dr. Livesey and Mr. Trelawney have asked me to write down the story of Treasure Island. I am glad to do so. I shall write the whole story from the beginning to the end. However, I cannot tell you where Treasure Island is, because some treasure is still there. I myself shall never go back there. Never! Once is enough for me!

The story begins in the year 1760. My father was then the inn-keeper at the Admiral Benbow Inn. I was a strong lad of fifteen. I helped my father who was then a very sick man.

One cold winter's day, an old seaman knocked at the inn-door and called for a glass of rum. He stood drinking it, in the doorway, looking out towards the sea.

"This is a nice, quiet spot," he said. "Do many people come here?

"Very few, I'm sorry to say," my father told him.

The old seaman finished his rum. "This is the place for me," he said. "I'll stay here." Then he shouted to a boy who was pushing a truck with his sea-chest on it, "Carry that upstairs!" He rubbed his hands, like a man well satisfied. He began to sing in a high, shaking voice:

> "Fifteen men on the dead man's chest,
>
> Yo—ho—ho, and a bottle of rum!"

We were always glad to have a guest in the inn, but we did not like this seaman at all. We were afraid of him. His appearance was fierce. He had a white scar down his right cheek. He was dirty and his clothes were torn. He almost never spoke to anybody—till he was drunk. Every evening he was drunk, and when he was drunk he would tell wild stories of wicked deeds—of murder, robbery, vengeance, and death. Everybody in the inn had to

listen. If not, he would draw his knife. "I'll cut your throat!" he would say. "I'll tear your heart out!" My father feared that he would drive all respectable people away from the inn. But no, the villagers still came as before. Although they were afraid of the seaman, they liked the excitement of his stories.

Our guest never paid my father for his boarding and lodging. My poor father was afraid to ask him for payment. He never told us his name. "Call me `Captain'. That will do," he said.

It was not long before I discovered that the Captain himself was afraid of something. He spent most days walking by the sea. He used to stand on a high rock, looking out to sea through his spy-glass. When he came home in the evening, he used to ask, "Has any seaman been here? Have you seen any seaman on the road?" He said to me once, "Jim, you're a smart lad. Keep a close watch all the time. If you see a seaman with only one leg, tell me at once. I'll give you a shilling on the first of every month for your trouble." He never kept his promise. And I, although I kept my eyes open, never saw any one-legged seaman near the inn.

The captain was afraid of Dr. Livesey too. The doctor had to come quite often to the inn because my

poor father grew weaker as the weather grew worse. One evening both Dr. Livesey and the captain were in the parlour. The captain had been drinking heavily, as usual. He was shouting his wicked tales and using dirty language.

"Stop that!" cried the doctor sharply.

The captain looked at him fiercely, drew his knife and threatened to throw it at the doctor. There was dead silence in the inn-parlour. The villagers dared not speak or move. Dr. Livesey's voice broke the silence. He said quietly but firmly, "I have two things to say to you. First, if you go on drinking rum as you are doing you'll soon be dead. Secondly, if you don't stop your wicked talk, I'll make a complaint. I'm a magistrate as well as a doctor, and I mean what I say. You'll be hanged if you go on like this."

The captain stared at him fiercely. Then his eyes dropped and he fell silent. For many evenings after that, he was unusually quiet. He did not stop his drinking but he stopped his wicked talk.

# 2

# BLACK DOG ARRIVES

That winter was unusually cold. My poor father grew worse every day. My mother nursed him. I looked after the inn as well as I could. One cold January morning, I was getting breakfast ready for the captain. He had gone out early for a walk along the beach. I was laying the table when a seaman came to the door. He was a thin, weak, yellow-faced man. Two fingers of his left hand were missing.

"Is that table for my mate, Bill Bones?" he asked.

"Bill Bones... I don't know .... It's the captain's table.

"Ah, the captain! That's right. The captain has a scar down his right cheek, hasn't he?"

"Yes," I said.

"Where is he?

"He's gone for a walk... that way...." I

said, going to the door and pointing to the beach.

The stranger pulled me back inside the parlour. "You stay here with me, my lad," he said.

I went on laying the table. He stood by the window, looking out.

"Here he comes!" he cried suddenly. "Get behind that door." He pushed me behind the door and stood beside me. "We'll give Bill a nice surprise," he said. He held my arm with fingers that were like iron."

The captain walked in, banged the door, and marched to his table.

"Hey! Bill," shouted the stranger.

The captain turned. All the colour left his face. I felt a sudden pity for him. He looked suddenly old and ill.

"Well, Bill, 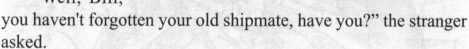 you haven't forgotten your old shipmate, have you?" the stranger asked.

"Black Dog!" the captain said breathlessly.

"That's me. Black Dog. And I've come to see my old shipmate. Billy Bones. We've had some happy times together, haven't we?"

"What do you want?" the captain growled.

"First, I'd like a glass of rum. Then we'll have a little talk about old times, won't we? Fetch the rum, boy!"

I fetched the rum. Then Black Dog sent me away. I went to the bar where I could not hear what they said. Soon they began to shout and to quarrel. Crash! The chairs and the table were being knocked over. The two men were fighting.

Black Dog ran past me, bleeding from a wound in his left shoulder. The captain was at his heels, ready to strike again, but Black Dog was the faster of the two. Like a hare, he ran off down

the road and over the hill.

The captain came back inside. "Jim," he said to me, "bring me a glass of rum." As he spoke, he nearly fell.

"Has he hurt you?" I asked anxiously.

"Rum, mate! Bring me that rum!" he answered. Then he added, "I must get away from here at once."

I ran to the bar. My hand was shaking so much that I broke a glass. I was filling a second glass, when I heard a "crash" in the parlour. I ran in. The captain had fallen to the floor. My mother, who had heard the noise, came rushing downstairs.

"What's the matter, Jim?" she asked. Then her eyes fell on the captain. His face had turned blue. His eyes were closed. He was breathing hard. "Oh!" she cried, "What shall we do? Your poor father upstairs is so ill. And now, this......"

Luckily, Dr. Livesey came in at that moment.

"Is he badly wounded?" my mother asked the doctor.

"Wounded? He's not wounded. It's his heart. I told him what would happen if he went on drinking ..... You go upstairs to your husband. Mrs. Hawkins, Jim and I will look after this fellow."

I held the basin while the doctor opened a vein and drew a lot of blood from the captain's arm. At last, the captain came to his senses. He looked around him. "Where's that Black Dog?" he cried.

"There's no black dog here," the doctor said. "It's the rum that you've been drinking. I told you what would happen. Now you must stop your drinking. Do you hear me? Rum means death to you."

Dr. Livesey and I helped the captain upstairs. We put him to bed. "You must stay there a week," the doctor said to him, "and no rum!" Then the doctor went to see my poor father.

**3**

# THE BLACK SPOT

Later, I went to give the captain his medicine. "Jim," he said, "you've always been a friend to me. Fetch me a glass of rum!"

"The doctor said...." I began.

"The doctor knows nothing about men like us.... I must have it, Jim. I'll pay you in gold, I will, Jim. Fetch it! I tell you....." He began to shout. I did not want him to wake my father up, and so I fetched him a glass of rum.

He drank it quickly. "Ah! That's better," he cried. Then he went on, "I've got to get away from here quickly. They'll be coming for me at any mo-

ment. And they'll bring the Black Spot....."

"The Black Spot? What's that?"

"You'll see, mate. You'll see. I must get up. I must be ready for them when they come...." He tried to sit up but he could not. "The doctor has killed me," he said.

For a time, he lay there quietly, collecting his strength. Then he began to speak again. He spoke so quickly and his words were so strange that I hardly understood him. "You've seen Black Dog," he said. "The others are worse than he. The man with one leg is the worst of all. They want my sea-chest. They're after the map and the money. When they come, Jim, run for the doctor. Tell him to bring a dozen men with him. If he does, he'll catch all Flint's men. I was on old Flint's ship. He left the map with me. I'm the only one who knows... Do what I tell you, Jim. You...." His voice grew weaker. His mind began to wander. He stopped speaking. I gave him his medicine. Almost at once he fell asleep. I left the room.

That evening my poor father died. My mother and I were very sad. We were very busy too, for many neighbours came to visit us. We had also to arrange everything for the funeral. I had little time to look after the captain.

He came downstairs and sat in the parlour. He looked very ill and he ate very little. All the same, he drank his rum as usual. On the night before the funeral, he was shamefully drunk. My poor father was lying dead upstairs while the parlour rang with his wild singing:

"Fifteen men on the dead man's chest —

Yo—ho—ho, and a bottle of rum!

Drink and the devil had done for the rest —

Yo—ho—ho—, and a bottle of rum!"

On the afternoon after the funeral, I was standing in the door-way of the inn. I was feeling very sad over my father. Then I heard the "tap—tap—tap" of a stick on the road. I looked up and saw a strange figure coming towards me. It was an old, blind man, bent with years or with illness. When he came nearer, I saw

his face. It was so evil that I felt frightened. The man stopped and asked:

"Will any kind friend tell a poor, blind man the way to the Benbow Inn?"

"You're just in front of it," I told him.

"Thank you, kind gentleman. Will you kindly give me your hand and lead me inside?" I gave him my hand. He held it with iron fingers. I tried to pull it away but he twisted my arm. "I'll break your arm for you if you don't do what I ask," he said in a cold cruel, evil voice. "Take me to the captain!"

"But....." I began.

He twisted my arm cruelly. "No `buts'. Just march. Take me

to him. Say, `Here's a friend come to see you, Bill.' Do you under-stand me?" He gave another twist to my arm.

I led him to the captain. "Here's a friend come to see you, Bill," I cried.

The captain looked up. He turned as white as a sheet. He tried to stand up and then he fell back into his chair.

"Well, old shipmate, here I am with the message you were expecting," the blind man said to the captain. Then he said to me, "Give me his hand." I brought the captain's left hand near. The stranger put something into it. Then he turned and left the inn quickly. I heard his stick "tap-tapping" along the road. The captain and I seemed turned to stone. I was the first to move. I dropped the captain's hand. He looked at the message that the blind man had left in it.

"The Black Spot!" he screamed. He sprang to his feet. "They're coming at ten o'clock. I still have six hours. I'll get away. They won't catch me. No! No!" Then he fell to the floor—dead!

**4**

# THE SEA-CHEST

M y mother at once sent a boy to fetch Dr. Livesey.

"We must leave the inn at once," I told her. "We're in danger here. They're coming for him at ten o'clock to-night. They want his sea-chest.

There's money in it and a map."

"If there's money," said my mother, "some of it belongs to us. He's paid us nothing since he's been here. I'll take what he owes us. It belongs to you, Jim, my poor, fatherless boy...." My poor mother began to cry.

"Your're right, mother," I said. Then I locked all the doors. I bent

down over the dead man. A piece of paper had fallen from his hand. The Black Spot! On one side of it was a black spot. On the other, was written this message: "We shall come at ten o'clock tonight." I began to search the captain's pockets for the key to his sea-chest. I found many things: a knife, some tobacco, a small compass, a needle and thread. The key was not there.

"Perhaps he carries it round his neck," my mother said.

Yes, there was the key, hanging on a dirty piece of string. My mother lit a candle and we went upstairs to the captain's room.

"Give me the key," my mother said. She walked straight to the chest. She opened it. A strong smell of tobacco came out. On the top lay a new suit of clothes. Under that, we found many different things: tobacco, pistols, a gold watch, a fan, some sea-shells.

There was no money. I pulled out a heavy coat, white with salt and smelling of the sea. Under that was a bag full of money and a small packet wrapped in cloth.

"I shall take what he owes me, and not a penny more," said my mother. "I'll show those thieves that I'm an honest woman." She began taking gold coins out of the money-bag. This took a long time, for most of the coins were foreign ones. We had to look for the English coins.

We were separating the coins when I heard a sound that frightened me. "Tap—tap—tap". It was the blind man's stick on the road! The sound came nearer and nearer. The stick banged loudly on the door. The door was roughly shaken. Then we heard "tap—tap—tap" again. The blind man was going away from the inn. My mother and I breathed again!

"Take it all, mother! Let's go!"

"No! I shall take just what he owes us. It isn't seven o'clock yet. There's still time." She began counting again.

There was no time. We heard a whistle coming from the sea, not far away.

"Come on, mother!"

She was already on her feet, ready to run. "This will have to

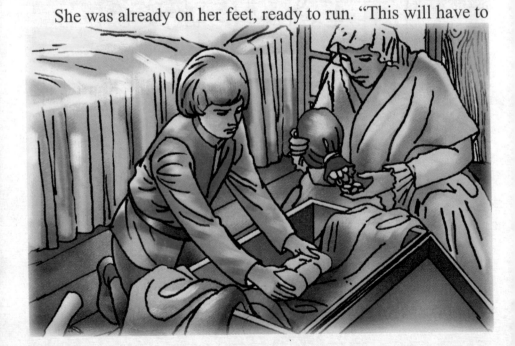

do. I'll just take this," she said, putting a small heap of coins into her bag.

"And I'll take this," I said, picking up the small packet wrapped in cloth.

We left the candle where it was. We went quickly down the dark stairs, and out into the road. A thick mist covered the inn. That was lucky for us. Through the mist, not far away, we caught the sound of running feet. Hand in hand, we made our way towards the village.

We had not gone far before my mother stopped and said, "Jim, you must run on with the money. I can't go a step farther. I'm going to faint." As she spoke, she almost fell. What could we do now? Those footsteps sounded very near. I looked round me desperately. Ah! The bridge. There was a bridge nearby and I half-carried my mother to it. Roughly, I pushed her under it, and followed her myself. There we both hid. It was not a minute too soon. The men had nearly reached the inn.

# 5

# BLIND PEW MEETS A HORRIBLE END

I was eager to see what was going to happen. Accordingly, I crept from under the bridge and into some bushes by the road side. From there, I saw nine or ten men fast approaching the inn. A man with a lamp ran first. Then came three men together. Hand in hand they ran, with the blind man in the middle. They reached the inn.

"Break the door down!" shouted the blind man.

His two companions rushed at the door to break it down. I heard their cries of surprise when they found the door unlocked.

"Get inside!" the blind man shouted. Four or five of the men rushed inside the inn, two remained in the road with their blind companion. Then, from the parlour, came the shout:

"Bill's here. He's drunk.... No! He's dead!"

"Search him! Get the key!" the blind man shouted.

I heard heavy feet rushing up the stairs. A window in the captain's room was thrown open. A rough voice shouted:

"Pew! Somebody has been here before us. They've opened the chest."

"Is it there?"

"The money's here."

"And Flint's paper?"

"They're gone!"

"Search Bill. They may be on him."

"We've searched him. They're not there."

"That boy and his mother have taken them. They were here when I came before. Find that boy, lads! Find him—and I'll tear his eyes out. Search! Go on! Search!" Pew was shaking with anger and disappointment. He struck the road with his stick, shouting wildly, "search! I tell you search!"

The men came out of the inn. "We've searched everywhere. It's no use, Pew. The papers have gone."

At that moment, a low whistle rang out twice from the direction of the sea. It was clearly a signal of alarm. Three of the men ran off at once. The others stood there, waiting for blind Pew.

"You dogs!" shouted the blind man. "Those papers mean thousands and thousands of pounds. They'll make us rich—rich as kings. And you won't stop to search. That boy can't be far away. Find him you dogs!" He began to strike out at his companions with his stick. He was mad with rage.

"Come on, Pew. We've got the money. Let's go while we can."

"Go!" Pew screamed, like a madman. "Go! You dogs!" He hit out wildly. His companions tried to pull his stick away from him. My heart felt sick at that wild sight.

To my joy, there came then the sound of a pistol shot and galloping horses. The men ran

away in different directions, leaving the blind man alone. Pew ran up and down the road, crying, "Johnny, Black Dog, Dick— you won't leave old Pew behind—not your old shipmate, Pew— poor, old blind Pew!

By the light of the moon, I could see five horsemen galloping down the hill. Pew heard them. He ran to the side of the road and fell into the dry bed of the stream. Quickly he pulled himself up, and then he ran back to the road, screaming horribly. He ran straight in front of the galloping horses. Down he fell. The riders tried to stop but they could not. Their horses galloped over blind Pew's body.

I jumped out of my hiding-place and ran towards the riders. I knew them well and they knew me. They were Captain Dance and his men, all customs-officers, whose duty was to look out for pirates.

"Why! Jim, my lad, what's the matter?" Captain Dance asked me.

I told him all that had happened. Then he asked, "What were they after? Money?"

"Yes. Money and some papers. They didn't find the papers because I have them here. I'd like to hand them over to Dr. Livesey, sir."

"That's right. Livesey is the magistrate and he should have them. I have to go and see him too. I must tell him about that fellow in the road. Jump up on my horse, Jim! We'll go togther."

I got up on Dance's horse and rode behind him to Livesey's house.

**6**

# FLINT'S TREASURE

D r. Livesey's house was in darkness. I knocked and Captain Dance shouted till, at last, a sleepy maid came to the door. "Dr. Livesey's out," she told us. "He's gone to spend the evening with Mr. Trelawney."

Mr. Trelawney was the most important man of the district. He was the Squire of our village. The villagers held him in great respect. They said that he had a large room filled from the floor to the ceiling with books and that he could read them all! He was also a great traveller. Never had I thought that one day, I, Jim Hawkins, the innkeeper's son,

would meet him, and even talk to him.

We found the doctor at Mr. Trelawney's. Both men were sitting by the fire, smoking. It was true—the room was full of books! Mr. Trelawney rose as we came in. He was a tall, stout man, with a red face. "Why, Dance!" he cried, "What brings you here?" Then Captain Dance stood up very straight and told his story. The two gentlemen listened with such interest that they forgot to smoke. "You are a brave fellow, Dance," Mr. Trelawney said "You've done well in riding down that black pirate, Pew." Then he turned to me, and said, "Come here, Jim Hawkins. Let me take a look at you." I came forward and stood up straight. "A brave lad," he said to me. "Now, Dance, a glass of wine before you go." Captain Dance drank his wine and went away.

When he had gone, the doctor said to me. "Jim, let me see that packet, will you?" I handed him the packet and he put it on the table in front of him.

"You've heard of Captain Flint, sir, haven't you?" he asked the Squire.

"Heard of him? Who hasn't? He was the most blood-thirsty pirate of them all."

"Have you heard of his treasure?"

"I've heard of that too. He buried it before he died, but nobody knows where."

"These papers may tell us where," the doctor said quietly.

"If they do, then I'll buy a ship and we'll go and find it—you and I and young Hawkins here."

"Well, then, we'll open Jim's packet. Fetch me the scissors from my bag, Jim."

The doctor cut the packet open. Inside was a small book and a piece of paper.

"We'll look at the book first," the doctor said.

On the first page of the book was written the name "Billy Bones". Then there were a dozen pages that had dates on them. Each date was followed by a figure and the name of a place. Like this, for

example: "June 12th, 1745. 170. Trinidad."

"I see what it is," cried Mr. Trelawney excitedly. "It's the account book of that black-hearted pirate, Billy Bones. On that date, they sank a ship at that place. He got that sum of money as his share."

"You're right, sir," said the doctor. "This book shows what he earned in twenty years. Whew!

Who would believe it...."

At the end of the book was a list showing the value of French and Spanish coins in English money.

"And now," said the doctor, "we'll take a look at that paper."

The Squire and I leaned over his shoulder and looked.

It was a map. It was the map of Treasure Island. Lines of latitude and longitude showed its exact position. Its length was about nine miles and its width about five. A smaller island lay to the south of it. This was called Skeleton Island. A large part of Treasure Island was forest-land. Part of it was swamp. Several hills were marked on the map. The highest was named "Spy-glass Hill". How our eyes shone when we saw three red crosses on the map! At the side of one were the words: "Here are the guns". At the side of the second was written: "Here are the silver bars". Beside the third: "Here is the treasure".

"Flint's treasure!" cried the Squire in great excitement.

"That is what the pirates are after," said the doctor.

The Squire was very excited. He got up and began to walk about, restlessly.

Treasure Island

"Here, wait a moment! There's something written on the back," the doctor cried.

On the back of the paper was written:

Tall tree, Spy-glass shoulder, bearing a point to the N. of N.N.E.

Skeleton Island E.S.E. and by E.

Ten feet.

The bar silver is in the north hole. You can find it by the line of the east rise, ten fathoms south of the black rock.

The arms are easy to find, in the sand-hill, N. point of north inlet cliff, bearing E. and a quarter N.

"I don't know what that means," said the Squire. "But we shall find out when we get there. I'm going to Bristol at once. I'm going to buy a ship. Doctor, you must find somebody to do your work. You'll be our ship's doctor. Hawkins, you'll be cabin-boy. Three of my men—Redruth, Joyce, and Hunter—will come too."

"I'll come with you gladly. And I know Hawkins will," the doctor said, looking at my joyful face. "But we must be careful, very careful. It will be a dangerous adventure. The pirates are our enemies. They'll do all they can to stop us. It'll mean fighting. It'll mean death. And there's one man I'm really afraid of... ."

"Who? Who?" the Squire asked. "Tell me who and I'll shoot him down like a dog."

"You."

"Me!"

"Yes, you. We must keep this matter secret. Nobody must know that we're going after treasure. You can't keep a secret. You'll be telling everybody."

"Livesey, I won't say a word, not a word. I'll be as silent as the grave," the Squire promised.

# 7

# WE ARE READY TO SAIL

The very next day, the Squire went to Bristol. Dr. Livesey set out for London to find a doctor to take his place. They left me at the Squire's house, the Hall, under the care of old Redruth, the gardener. "You must stay here and not go out," they told me, "be careful! The pirates are after you!" My mother was not anxious about me. She was staying in the village with some friends of hers.

I spent my time in day-dreams. By night and by day, I dreamt of adventures on Treasure Island. My dreams were all delightful ones. I had no idea of the fearful dangers that awaited me.

It was not long before a letter arrived from the Squire. The letter was addressed to Dr. Livesey: "If absent, to be opened by Redruth or Hawkins". Accordingly, Redruth and I opened it. I read it out to Redruth:

The Anchor Inn,

Bristol.

March 1st.

Dear Livesey,

I don't know whether you're at the Hall or in London. I'm writing to you at both places.

"You'll be glad to know that I've bought a fine ship, the Hispaniola by name. People here have been most helpful, especially when they knew that we were sailing after treasure." I stopped reading and exclaimed, "The Squire has been talking! Dr. Livesey won't like that." Then I continued :

"I've been lucky over the crew too. At first it was hard to find suitable seamen. I was able to find six but that was all. Then, by chance, I met an old sailor who used to serve as a ship's cook. He brought me luck. Since meeting him, everything has gone well. He found the rest of the crew for me. They don't look very pretty, it's true. All the same, they look strong enough to fight a warship. The ship's cook, who has been such a help to me, is called Long John Silver. The poor fellow has only one leg."

Again I stopped reading. "The poor fellow has only one leg" I repeated to myself. At once I thought of Billy Bones and his fear of the seaman with one leg. I said nothing to Redruth however. I went on with my reading:

"I am very well. I eat like a

wolf. I sleep like a log. Never have I felt better.

"Do come as quickly as you can. I'm very eager to start. Everything is ready. The sea is calling me! Seaward ho! Come at once, if you can. You'll find me here at the Anchor Inn.

Hoping to see you very soon."

Yours sincerely,

John Trelawney.

P.S. Let young Hawkins spend his last day with his mother. Redruth will have to be with him all the time.

J.T.

I went with Redruth to the Admiral Benbow Inn. I am glad to say that I found my mother well and cheerful. The furniture broken by the pirates had been repaired. The Squire had paid the bill for the repairs. He had bought a new armchair for my mother. Besides that, he had found a boy to help my mother while I was away.

I was glad to leave my mother and the old Benbow Inn that was so full of memories. It is not easy to leave the place where you were born! However, the

thought of Treasure Island excited and delighted me.

Redruth and I went by coach to Bristol. I remember almost nothing of that journey for I slept the whole way. When I woke up, the coach had stopped in a city street. I rubbed my eyes and asked, "Where are we, Tom?"

"In Bristol. Come on, Jim! Get out!"

I got out of the coach and walked along the quay with Redruth. The harbour delighted me. There were ships of all kinds of all nations. There were also seamen of all kinds and of all nations. There was a strong smell of salt and tar. I breathed deeply. This was the life for a boy like me! I too was going to sail far away. I was going to sail to Treasure Island. I was going to look for treasure. I felt that I was the luckiest boy in the world.

Squire Trelawney was standing in front of the Anchor Inn. He was wearing the uniform of a ship's officer. He was walking and talking like a ship's officer.

"Hurry up!" he cried to us. "The doctor's here already. Everything is ready."

"When are we sailing, sir?" I asked him.

"Tomorrow, at dawn."

"Hurrah!"

# 8

# A STRANGE HAPPENING AT THE SPY-GLASS INN

"Tomorrow at dawn!" Magic words! In twenty hour's time, we should be sailing to Treasure Island on the good ship *Hispaniola*. I was too excited to eat, I pushed my plate away. "Is there anything I can do, sir?" I asked Mr. Trelawney.

"Yes. Take this note to John Silver at the Spy-glass Inn," the Squire said. "Follow the quay. It's about a ten minutes' walk."

I was glad to walk along the quay once more. The Spy-glass Inn was easy to find. It had a brass spy-glass hanging outside as its sign. It was bright, clean, and cheerful place. The paint was fresh and the windows had neat, red curtains in them. I looked in. It was filled with seamen, talking, drinking rum and smoking.

As I was

looking, Long John Silver himself came from the bar with a tray of glasses of rum. His leg had been cut off at the top. All the same, with the help of his crutch, he moved about very quickly. Here and there he went, hopping like a bird at times. He smiled and whistled and, now and then, shouted a merry greeting. Was Long John the pirate whom Billy Bones had feared? I looked at his face. Impossible! His face was pleasant, friendly, and full of good-will. It was very different from the face of Billy Bones or that of Black Dog or of blind Pew. No! Long John Silver could not be a pirate.

I walked in. Long John was joking with a customer. I went straight up to him.

"Mr. Silver, sir?" I asked, handing him the note from the Squire.

"Yes. And who are you, my lad?"

"I'm the new cabin-boy, sir."

He opened the note and read it. `It's from Mr. Trelawney of the *Hispaniola*," he said. He spoke loudly. Then suddenly, a man got up in a hurry and left the inn. I looked at him as he passed. It was Black Dog!

"Stop him!" I shouted. "It's Black Dog!"

"After him, Ben!", cried Long John. "He hasn't paid for his rum." Then he turned to me and asked, "Who did you say he was?"

"Black Dog, sir. He's a pirate."

"A pirate! In my inn!" He called to the man who had been sitting with Black Dog. "Come here, Tom Morgan!" Morgan went up to him. "You've never seen that fellow before, have you?" asked Silver. "You didn't know that fellow's name, did you?"

"No, sir."

"You didn't know he was a pirate?"

"No, sir."

Ben came running back, breathless. He had not been able to catch Black Dog.

"I'll go and explain to Mr. Trelawney," Silver said to me. "What will he think! Pirates in my inn! This is a serious matter." Silver seemed very upset. "Come, boy! We'll go at once."

Silver walked back to the Anchor Inn with me. He was an interesting and cheerful companion. As he walked along the quay, he told me about the ships in the harbour: where they had come from, their cargo and their crews. "How lucky I am to have Long John as a shipmate!" I thought to myself.

At the Anchor Inn, we found Mr. Trelawney and Dr. Livesey enjoying a glass of beer. Silver told them what had happened in the Inn. He told his story truthfully. From time to time, he turned to me, asking, "That's how it was, wasn't it, Hawkins?"

"Yes, sir," I said.

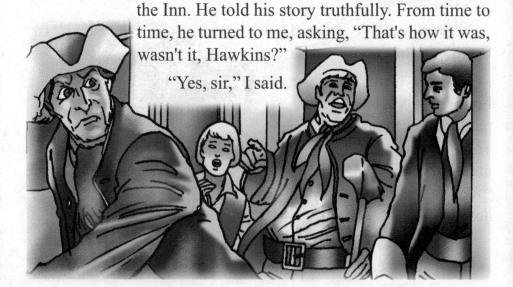

We were all sorry that Black Dog had got away. The Squire spoke for us all when he said, "It's pity. But you did everything you could, Silver. It wasn't your fault."

As Silver was going away, the Squire shouted after him, "All hands on board by four this afternoon!"

"Ay! Ay! Sir," Silver answered cheerfully.

"There goes an honest man," the doctor said. "I haven't much faith in your judgement, Squire, but you've done well in choosing Silver."

"Silver's just the man for us. I thought so from the start," the Squire said, looking very pleased.

I said nothing but I agreed with both of them.

"And now," the doctor said, "it's time for us to go on board. May Hawkins come along with us, Squire?"

"Yes," answered Mr. Trelawney. "Come along, Hawkins. You shall see the ship."

Joyfully I took my hat and followed them outside.

# 9

# CAPTAIN SMOLLETT EXPECTS TROUBLE

The Hispaniola lay at anchor some distance from the shore. A small boat took us out to the ship. As we climbed on board, we were met by the mate. This was Mr. Arrow, a brown, old sailor, with large ear-rings. "A good fellow," the Squire said as we went below to his cabin. The Squire seemed to like the mate. He certainly did not like the captain.

Hardly had we got down to the cabin when a sailor knocked at the door. "Captain Smollett is asking to see you, sir."

"Show him in."

The captain, who was close behind the sailor, came in. He shut the door carefully behind him. He looked angry.

"Well, Captain Smollett? All is well, I hope. All ship-shape and seaworthy?" "Sir, I must be frank with you. I don't like this voyage. I don't like the crew, and I don't like the mate.

"Perhaps, sir, you don't like the ship?" the Squire asked looking very angry.

"I can't say yet, sir. I haven't sailed her yet. She looks a good ship....."

"Perhaps you don't like your employer," the Squire asked, getting more and more angry.

A quarrel seemed likely.

"Here.... wait a minute!" Dr. Livesey cried. "We don't want any ill-will. Let the Captain explain! Captain Smollett, you've said that you don't like the voyage. Will you tell us why?"

"I agreed to sail this ship wherever Mr. Trelawney ordered. He told me nothing of his plans. Now I find that every man on board knows where we're going. Every sailor knows more than I do about the voyage. That's not fair."

"You're right, Captain Smollett; it's not fair," the doctor agreed. In your

place, I should feel as angry as you."

"Next," Captain Smollett went on, "I'm told by my own crew that we're going after treasure. That's a dangerous business. It's dangerous even when it is kept secret. But there's no secret about this voyage. Somebody has told the secret. Everybody knows it."

"We know that it's dangerous and we're ready for danger," the doctor told him. Then he asked, "You say that you don't like the crew. Why not? Aren't they good seamen?"

"I don't like them, sir," Captain Smollett repeated. "Mr. Trelawney should have allowed me to choose my crew."

"Perhaps you're right. And you don't like the mate?"

"I don't. He's too friendly with the men and he's too fond of drinking."

"Well now, will you tell us what you want?" Dr. Livesey said.

"Are you gentlemen determined to go on this voyage?"

"We are, sir," the Squire said firmly.

"Very well. Before we sail, two things should be done. First, the guns should be stored near your cabins. Secondly, your men,

Mr. Trelawney, should have their berths near your cabin."

"Then you're thinking that there will be mutiny on board?" Dr. Livesey asked.

"I haven't said so," the captain answered quickly. "If I thought so, I should have no right to sail. I am responsible for the safety of the ship and of every man on board . Therefore, I must ask you to be careful. I must take no risks. I must ask you to take no risks. It is my duty to do so."

"I agree with you," the doctor said.

"Yes," the Squire said, "we shall be careful. We shall do what you advise. But I'm sure that  the crew are better than you think."

"We shall see, sir," replied the captain. "I hope you are right. However, I must do my duty. That is all I have to say. Good day to you, gentlemen." Captain Smollett left the cabin.

When I went up on deck, later, I saw the crew moving the guns and the gun-powder. The captain and Mr. Arrow were standing there watching them.

"Ship ahoy!" Long John and the last of the crew arrived in a small boat. The cook climbed into the ship like a monkey. His quickness amazed me. He stopped to ask a seaman, "What's going on?"

"We're moving the guns and the gun-powder."

"That will make us late in starting. We'll miss the morning tide," Silver said.

"They are my orders," Captain Smollett told him sharply. "Go below, my man. The men will be wanting their supper."

"Ay! Ay! Sir," the cook answered cheerfully, going below to his galley.

I was tired but I could not leave the deck. I stayed there all that night. Everything there was so interesting: the sharp commands, the sharper whistle, the men working busily in the dim light of the lamps. Then, as the dawn came, the men cried, "A song! Let's have a song! Give us a start, Barbecue!" they called to the cook. Then Long John Silver or Barbecue—as his companions called him—began :

"Fifteen men on the dead man's chest—

Yo—ho—ho, and a bottle of rum."

That song took me back to the Benbow Inn. I could almost hear the voice of Billy Bones!

The anchor was pulled up. The wind filled the sails. The morning tide carried us easily out to sea. The good ship Hispaniola had begun her voyage to Treasure Island!.

# 10

# WE ARE ON OUR WAY TO TREASURE ISLAND

I shall not give all the details of our voyage to Treasure Island. The weather favoured us. There were several storms but the ship proved herself strong and seaworthy. Captain Smollett was pleased with her. The crew worked hard and well. However, two or three things happened which I must write down.

Mr. Arrow, the mate, turned out to be worse than Captain Smollett had feared. He let the men do just what they liked. Worst of all, he drank heavily. He was

nearly always drunk. Often he was unable to work. As an officer, he was useless. Certainly, he was a bad example to the men. One stormy night, he disappeared. He fell overboard. Nobody was sorry. Job Anderson took his place. Anderson was helped by Israel Hands, a careful and experienced seaman.

The most popular man on board was Long John Silver, or Barbecue as he was called. The men respected him and even obeyed him. "He's no ordinary man," Israel Hands said to me. "He's had a good schooling and he can talk like a book! And brave! Why! Barbecue's as brave as a lion. I've seen him knock four men down in a fight."

Everybody liked Long John. He was always cheerful and always had a pleasant word for everybody. He was very kind to me and I grew really fond of him. "Come into the galley Hawkins, and let's have a talk. You and me together," he would say to me. I often sat with him and his parrot, called *Captain Flint*. Long John kept the galley as clean as a new pin. His saucepans shone. His plates were in neat rows. Everything there was spotlessly clean and bright. There I would sit for hours, listening to his exciting

stories. Every now and then, Long John would turn to his parrot. "That's the truth. Cap'n, isn't it?" he would ask the bird. "Ah! Ay! Sir." the parrot would answer. "Ay! Ay! Sir. Ship ahoy! Seaward ho!" The parrot would repeat all this over and over again.Then Silver would throw his handkerchief over the cage to keep Captain Flint quite.

"That bird must be over two hundred years old," Silver told me once. "Parrots live for hundreds of years. Did you know that? Ah! He knows the smell of blood. The fighting and the wickedness that bird has seen! Eh, Captain Flint?" And the parrot would begin again: "Ay! Ay! Sir. Ship Ahoy! Seaward ho!"

Sometimes Silver would push a piece of sugar through the bars of the cage. The bird would eat it and then peck at the bars,

asking for more. Often he would swear in the most wicked way. "That comes from having been in bad company, Hawkins," Silver would say, "Keep away from bad company! Many a good lad had been ruined by bad companions."

I thought that Silver was the best of men. I liked him and I respected him. So did everybody else on board. However, before the end of the voyage, my opinion about him changed suddenly. I found him out. I found out what he really was. This is what happened:

It was the last day of our voyage. That night, or the following morning, we expected to reach Treasure Island. The sun had just set. My day's work was over. I was on my way to my berth when I thought I would like to eat an apple. I made my way to the apple barrel which stood on the deck. The barrel was almost empty. I had to climb down into it to reach an apple. I climbed down and sat there, enjoying one apple after another. I was tired and fell asleep.

How long I slept I do not know. Something hit the side of the barrel rather heavily. That awakened me. I was ready to jump up and climb out when I heard voices. I listened. What I heard made me stay where I was. I was nailed to the spot with horror!

# WHAT I OVERHEARD IN THE APPLE BARREL

Long John Silver was speaking. "I was in charge of the stores because of my leg. Ah! That doctor who cut it off was a clever fellow. All the same, he could do nothing of old Pew. He lost his sight in that same fight. Well, I knew we should have bad luck. I told them so. A ship's name should never be changed unless you want bad luck."

"Old Flint was always lucky," another voice said.

"Old Flint was the best man of the lot," another said.

"True," Silver agreed. "When I sailed with Flint, I got two thousand pounds. So did Billy

Bones. And so did old Pew. But they wasted theirs. I saved mine. Mine is safe in the bank. When I go back, I can live like a gentleman.

"Live like a gentleman!" said the voice of Israel Hands. "That's what I want. And I want it now. I want to taste that brandy that Smollett keeps in his cabin. It's time we did something, Barbecue. When are we going to begin? That's what I want to know."

"Now listen to me, Hands," said Silver. "Your head isn't of much use, but your ears are big enough. Listen! You'll work hard and talk soft, and keep off the drink till I give the word."

"That's what I am doing, isn't it?" Hands asked angrily. "What I'm asking is when you'll give the word."

"When? I'll tell you when. At the very last moment and not before that. We need the captain because he must steer the ship for us. We need the doctor and Mr. Trelawney because they have the map. Let them find the treasure. When the treasure's on board, then we'll act."

"What are we going to do with them?"

"There are two ways. Either leave them behind on the island or kill them."

"Kill them," said Israel Hands. "That was Billy Bones' way. 'Dead men don't bit,' he used to say."

"It's the best way," Silver agreed.

"John," cried Hands, "You're a man!"

"You'll say so, Israel, when you see. I ask only one thing.

Leave that Trelawney to me. I'll break his silly head!"

"And you leave Captain Smollett to me," Hands said. "I'm sick of his orders. I'll twist his neck like a chicken!"

"You shall, Israel, you shall," Silver promised. He stopped a moment and then he went on. "I'm thirsty. Dick, my lad, jump up and get me an apple."

You can think of my terror when I heard those words. I was too frightened to move. I simply sat there, waiting to be found out. I heard Dick stand up. I held my breath. Then Israel Hands cried out:

"If you're thirsty, have a drop of rum. Let's all have a drop."

"Here's the key, Dick," Silver said. "Fetch a bottle for us."

Dick soon came back. They began drinking. I heard them say, "Here's to luck!" "Here's to old Flint!" "Here's to us!"

Just then, a brightness fell over the barrel. I looked up. The moon had risen. The sails were shining like silver in the moonlight.

"Land-ho!" shouted the man on the look-out. "Land-ho!"

The good ship Hispaniola had reached Treasure Island.

# 12

## SIX MEN AND A BOY AGAINST NINETEEN PIRATES

I heard a rush of feet. Everyone was rushing to the side of the ship to look at the island. Quickly I climbed out of the barrel and joined the rest. I was trembling with excitement and fear. I was anxious to tell the Squire and the doctor what I had overheard. That was impossible in such a crowd. I had to wait for the right moment.

I looked ahead. The moon was shining bright over the

island. In the moonlight, I could see two low hills. Behind them was a higher hill whose peak was hidden in the mist. Captain Smollett gave an order. The ship sailed towards the east of the island.

"Has anybody seen that island before?" Captain Smollett asked his crew.

"I have, sir," Silver answered readily. "I was the cook on a ship that stopped here once for water."

"The best place for us to anchor is to the south, behind an islet, I think?"

"Yes, sir. Behind Skeleton Island. A man on board told me that the pirates always anchored there. They called that highest hill `the Spy-glass' because they kept a look-out man, with a spy-glass there."

"I have a map here," Captain Smollett said. "Take a look at it, will you?"

Silver's eyes burned in his head as he took the map. But the map was not Billy Bones'. It was a careful copy of it, without the red marks and the writing. Silver hid his diappointment. "Yes, sir," he said. "This is the spot. That's the bay where we anchored. We found plenty of fresh water there."

"Thank you, my man. I'll ask you later on to give us help. You may go."

Long John walked towards me. I was frightened of him now. I was sure that he did not know that I had been in the apple barrel. All the same, I felt both fear and hatred for the man. When he touched my shoulder, I trembled with horror.

"Ah," he said to me in the friendliest way, "you'll enjoy yourself on that island, Jim. You'll be able to bathe and climb trees. You'll be able to hunt the wild goats. You'll be running like a wild goat yourself. Ah! If I were young again, and with ten toes...."

After Silver had gone below to the galley, I went to where Dr. Livesey and the Squire were standing. I stood near them, waiting for an opportunity to speak to them. The doctor saw me. "Jim,"

he said, "run down to the cabin and fetch me my pipe." I did so. When I gave it to him, I said softly, "Doctor, please ask the Captain and Mr. Trelawney to go below. Then send for me. I have some terrible news to tell you."

The doctor said, as if he had asked me a question, "Thank you, Jim. That was all I wanted to know." He went to the Captain and Mr. Trelawney. The three gentlemen went on talking for a time. They showed no signs of surprise or dismay. Then the captain ordered all the crew on deck.

"My lads," he began, "I've a word to say to you. Our voyage has been a prosperous one. Every man has done his duty. I am satisfied. Mr. Trelawney, Dr. Livesey and I are now going below to drink to your good health and good luck. I've ordered rum to be served out to all of you. I want you to drink to our good health and good luck."

"Three cheers for Cap'n Smollett!" shouted Long John.

The crew gave three hearty cheers for the Captain. I could hardly believe that these same men were planning to kill him!

The three gentlemen went below. Soon afterwards, Captain Smollett sent for me. I found them sitting round the table on which was a bottle of Spanish wine. The doctor was smoking.

"Now, Hawkins," Mr. Trelawney said, "you have something to tell us. Speak up, my lad!"

I told them what I had overheard. They listened with great attention. Their eyes never left my face for a moment. When I had finished, they made me sit down at the table with them. They praised my courage and they drank to my good health. The Squire then turned to the Captain, "Captain Smollett," he began, "I beg your pardon. You were right and I was wrong. I am a fool."

"You're not more foolish than I am," Captain Smollett said. I can't understand this crew. When a crew means to mutiny, there's always some trouble before hand. Till now, I've found nothing to complain of. I just don't understand...."

"It's Silver who is keeping the men quiet. He's keeping them

quiet till the time for action comes. He is an unusual man..."

"Yes. Yes," Captain Smollett said impatiently. "But we're talking too much. We must think of action. I'd like to make three or four points, if Mr. Trelawney will allow me to."

"You, sir, are the captain. It is for you to speak," the Squire said.

"My first point is this," Captain Smollett then said. "We must go on because we can't turn back. If I give the order to turn back, there would be mutiny at once. Second point: we have time—at least till the treasure is found. Third point: some of the men are on our side. Your servants are, for certain, Mr. Trelawney?"

"Oh, certainly?"

"That's three. With us, that makes seven, counting Hawkins here. Now, are there any honest men among the others?"

"Perhaps there are some among those whom you chose, sir?" Dr. Livesey asked the Squire.

"No. Hands was one of my men."

"Well," the Captain went on, "at the moment, there's nothing we can do. We can only wait. Jim can help us more than anyone. He's a boy with a sharp eye. The men like him."

"Yes, Hawkins," the Squire said to me, "I have great faith in you."

I heard these words with dismay. I felt really helpless. Our position was desperate. Six men and a boy, against nineteen pirates !

# 13

# THE PIRATES LAND ON TREASURE ISLAND AND SO DO I!

Early the next morning, I was on deck, looking at Treasure Island. The ship lay half a mile to the S.E. of the coast. She was rolling so heavily that I felt sick. Was it this that made me feel I hated the island? Or was it the sight of the sad, green woods and the sad crying of the sea-gulls? I don't know, but from the start I hated the island.

The heat was terrible. There was no wind. There was not a breath of air. The men complained fiercely over their work as they brought the ship to anchor. We anchored in

the narrow channel between Treasure Island and the islet called Skeleton Island. We were about half-way from either shore.

The woods came right down to the sea. There was a heavy smell of wet leaves and rotting trees. The doctor smelt the air, like somebody smelling a bad egg. "I don't know whether there's any treasure here or not," he said. "But I'm certain that there's malaria."

The men lay on the deck, exhausted by the heat. Some were whispering together. All of them were grumbling. All orders were received with black looks. All commands were obeyed carelessly and unwillingly. At any moment the mutiny might begin. We were quick to see the danger. So was Silver. He went hopping from one

group of men to another. I knew he was advising them to be patient. But he was clearly anxious, that seemed to us a bad sign.

Captain Smollett decided to send the men ashore. "If I give another order, there'll be a mutiny," he explained to us. "Silver can save us. He wants the men to wait. Let him go ashore with the men. Let him talk to them. They'll come back as quiet as lambs."

We agreed with him. We had to, because we could think of no other plan.

Captain Smollett then spoke to the men. "My lads," he said, "we've had a hot day and we're all tired. A walk on shore will be good for everybody. Those who want to can go on shore. They can stay there till sunset. I'll fire the gun half an hour before sunset."

At once the men forgot their tiredness and their anger. They thought that they would find the treasure as soon as they landed.

They gave a loud cheer and prepared the ship. Silver was in command. He left six of his men on the ship. The remaining thirteen got into two boats.

The boats were ready to start when suddenly I had an idea. It was a mad idea but, in the end, it helped to save us. I decided that I would go on shore with the pirates. I jumped into the first boat as it was leaving.

The two boats raced for the beach. The boat I was in got there first. Before it touched the  beach, I had caught the branch of a tree and had swung myself on to the shore. Then I ran off into the bushes. I heard Silver shouting, "Jim! Jim!". That made me run even faster. Jumping, falling breaking through the bushes, I ran on till I could run no farther.

# 14

# I EXPLORE AND AM FRIGHTENED ALMOST TO DEATH

I stopped, breathless, and then I looked round me. I had run through a swamp with its bushes and low trees. Now I was on the edge of an open stretch of sandy country. Not far off, was a high hill with two peaks to it. I began to enjoy myself.

I was very pleased that I had got away from Long John and his men. Besides, I felt the joy of the explorer. Here was I, Jim Hawkins, in an uninhabited island. This was my island and I was the King.

That feeling did not last long. Suddenly a wild duck rose up from the bushes not

far away from me. With a frightened "quack", it flew high into the air. Hundreds of other ducks followed it. What had alarmed the birds? Somebody was coming. Was it Long John? My fears returned. I climbed up the nearest tree and waited there, as quiet as a mouse.

I heard voices and footsteps. Yes! It was Long John with another seaman. They stopped quite near my hiding-place.

"Listen, Tom!" Silver was saying in a friendly tone. "I'm telling you for your own good. If you don't join us, you're going to be sorry."

"That may be," Tom said, "But it's a wicked plan, Silver, and you know it. Why are you with that lot? You've got plenty of money. You're brave, I know that. You're honest—at least I thought so." Tom stopped for a moment and then he said, "No, Silver, I'm not joining you. I'll do my duty even if I die for it."

"Die for it you will, that's certain." Silver told him, in a very cruel tone.

A horrible scream rang out from far off. The wild ducks rose into the air and flew wildly overhead. The scream echoed among the rocks. It terrified me. It terrified poor Tom as well.

"What was that, John?" he asked in a shaking voice.

"That was Alan. They've killed him."

"God rest his soul!" Tom said. "He was a true seaman. No, Silver, kill me, but I'm not joining. Do your worst! I'll do my duty till the last...."

With these brave words, Tom turned to leave Silver. As soon as his back was turned. Silver acted. He threw his crutch with a terrible strength. It hit poor Tom in the middle of his back. With a cry, the brave fellow fell to the ground. In a second, Silver was on top of him, striking at him with his knife. I saw two savage blows. Then I think I nearly fainted. The world turned round and round. The trees, Silver, poor Tom—all went in a circle, round and round. For a moment, I thought that I was going to fall from the tree. That would have been the end of Jim Hawkins, the great explorer!

My faintness quickly passed. I looked down. Silver was standing by poor Tom. He was cleaning his knife on the grass. Then he put his hand into his pocket, took out a whistle and blew it sharply three times. Was that a signal for his men to come? Again I was filled with fear. Alan and Tom were already dead. They would kill me if they found me.

I crept down from the tree very quietly. I ran into the bushes. Silver was shouting to his men and they were answering. Their shouts were coming nearer. I left the bushes for the more open part of the wood. There I ran as I had never run before. Fear gave me wings. I did not know where I was running. I did not care.

My fears grew as I ran. I could not go back to the Hispaniola because the pirates had the boats. Their hands were already red with murder. They would murder me as soon as they saw me. I had to stay on the island. But there I would die of hunger. My thoughts were desperate ones. I ran on desperately. Then, at last, I found myself at the foot of the hill with the two peaks. Gasping for breath, I looked up, and saw a fresh danger!

# 15

# THE MAN OF THE ISLAND

Some stones came rolling down the side of the hill. Some body was up there, among the trees! I saw a figure run from one tree to the next. It was a strange figure. Dark and hairy it was. Was it a man or a monkey? Was it a wild man? I fled. The creature followed me. On and on I ran. The creature was

never far away. As fast as a hare it ran, its body bent almost double. But it moved, like a man, on two legs. "If it is a man, why am I afraid?" I asked myself. "I have my pistol."

I stopped running. I took my pistol from my belt and walked towards the creature. It came out from behind a tree-trunk, moved two or three steps towards me, and then stopped. It was a man! He threw himself on his knees in front of me. He clasped his hands and held them out to me. He seemed to be begging for mercy!

"Who are you?" I asked.

"Ben Gunn. I'm poor Ben Gunn, I am. I've lived here, all alone these three years. Three years—all by myself!"

He was a white man like myself but he had been burned black by the sun. His blue eyes looked strange in his dark face. His hair and beard were long and snow-white. His clothes were rags, held together by string or sticks.

"Three years!" I cried. "Were you shipwrecked?"

"No. I was marooned."

I began to feel very sorry for the poor fellow. Marooned! Left here alone by the pirates! Left here to die slowly of hunger—

although he had managed, somehow, to live on!

"Marooned," repeated Ben Gunn. "Three years ago. I've lived on wild goats, berries, and shell-fish. Ah! Wouldn't I like some proper food! You don't happen to have any cheese with you? Night after night, I've dreamt of cheese. What wouldn't I give for just a taste!"

"I'm sorry," I said, "I don't happen to have any cheese with me. But, if I get on board again, you shall have all the cheese you can eat."

Ben Gunn had been fingering the cloth of my coat and stroking my hands. He stopped suddenly and asked sharply, "Who's stopping you from going on board?"

"Not you, I know," I answered.

"Ah, no, not I.... What's your name, my lad?"

"Jim."

"Jim, Jim" he repeated. Then, in a rush, he told me: "Well, Jim, I've been living a rough life. But I was carefully brought up, I was. My mother was a good woman, Jim. She taught me to say my prayers.... then I went wrong, I did. And that brought me here. But I've been thinking. If ever I get off this island, I'm going to lead a good life. A good, holy life, Jim. I'm not going to touch rum. No! Well, may be, a little glass now and then......"

He stopped for breath. Then he whispered in my ear, "I'm rich, Jim! I'm rich!"

I was thinking that the poor fellow was mad. His loneliness must have made him mad. Perhaps he read my thoughts, for he said, angrily, "You don't believe me... but it's true. You were the first that found me, Jim, and I'll give you a share....."

A frightened look came over his face. "Jim," he said, "tell me the truth. You're not on Flint's ship, are you?"

I answered him readily for I felt that he was a friend.

"No, it's not Flint's ship. Flint is dead. But some of his men are on the ship, and that's bad for us."

"Is there.... is there a man with one leg?"

"Long John Silver?"

"Ay! That's his name."

"He's there. He's the cook and he's the leader of Flint's men."

All this time, Ben Gunn had been holding my hand. Now, he pressed it so hard that I almost cried out.

"You haven't come from Long John, have you? Tell me true, lad! If he's sent you, then it's the end of Ben Gunn...."

I decided to tell him the whole story of our voyage and our present danger. I did so. He listened with great interest. When I had finished, he stroked my hand.

"You're a good lad, Jim," he said. "You're in a nasty corner but we'll find a way out. Trust in Ben Gunn. Ben Gunn is the man. I'll help you, Jim." He paused a moment. Then he asked me, "Tell me, Jim, is your Mr. Trelawney likely to be generous to a man who helped him?"

"The Squire's a gentleman," I said, "and a generous man as well."

"Do you think that he'd let me have..... say..... a thousand pounds of the money... the money that's mine already?"

"I'm sure he would. He's promised all the men a fair share."

"And my passage home as well?"

"Of course. We'll need you to help us sail the ship home."

"That's true," he said, looking pleased. "So you will." He stroked my hand. Then he said, "Well, Jim, you've told me your story. Now, I'll tell you mine. I was on Flint's ship when he came here with the treasure. Billy Bones was the mate. Long John was in charge of the stores. Flint went on shore with six of the men. Big, strong fellows they were. After a week, he came back on board, alone. He'd buried the treasure—and killed the six fellows. He sailed away at once. Then, it happened that, three

years ago, I was on another ship and we saw this island. 'That's Flint's island,' I told my mates. 'Let's go and look for his treasure.' We looked for it for twelve days but we didn't find it. My shipmates were very angry with me. 'Here, Benjamin,' they said, here's a gun and an axe. We're leaving you here to find Flint's treasure.' They sailed away and left me here."

Ben Gunn stopped and asked me anxiously, "You'll speak to Mr. Trelawney for me, Jim, won't you?"

"Yes," I promised him. "But I don't know how I'm going to get back on board."

"You can have my boat, Jim. I made it myself, with my own two hands. It's lying there, just under the White Rock."

At that moment, we heard the sound of the ship's cannon—two hours before sunset!

"They're fighting!' I cried. "Come on, Ben!"

We jumped up and ran in the direction of the Bay. The cannon had stopped but guns were being fired. The fight had begun. We ran on in the direction of the ship.

I stopped suddenly. High above some trees, the English flag was flying.

"Your friends are there, Jim. You go on. I shan't come with you. If Mr. Trelawney or the other gentlemen want to see me, you know where to find me," Ben Gunn told me.

"Thank you, Ben," I said, running fast towards the flag.

# 16

# DR. LIVESEY CONTINUES THE STORY

The two boats left the Hispaniola at half past one. At that time, Captain Smollett, Mr. Trelawney and I were down below in the cabin. We were planning what to do. If there had been a wind, we should have attacked the six pirates on board. Then we should have sailed out to sea. But there was no wind. There was not a breath of air. The heat was suffocating. We felt helpless. We felt worse when Hunter told us that Jim Hawkins had gone to the island with the pirates. We did not doubt Jim's loyalty. But we were afraid for his safety.

We went up on deck and looked towards the island. The pirates had left their boats near the mouth of the river. In each boat there was a man on guard. I felt that I had to do something. Accordingly, Hunter and I got into the one remaining boat, and rowed for the island. We made for the stockade and landed about a hundred yards from it. This is what we saw :

The stockade was a house made of logs. It was strongly built and large enough to hold forty men. Each of its walls had loopholes for guns. Around the house, a wide space had been cleared of trees and bushes. All round this, there was a strong fence, built of logs, about six feet high. It was a perfect shelter. The people inside were perfectly safe from their enemies. There was a spring of pure water close to the house. The stockade was the place for us.

While Hunter and I were looking round, we heard a terrible scream. It was Alan's, but I learnt that only afterwards. At once I decided. We must bring stores and guns to the stockade and stay there.

Hunter and I rowed back to the ship. Both Captain Smollett and the Squire agreed with me. At once, we began loading the boat with stores and guns. The six pirates on board could do nothing to stop us. The captain was standing with two pistols at one end of the deck. Redruth was standing at the other end, similarly armed. Both were ready to shoot. The captain told the pirates, "Here are two of us, with a couple of pistols each. If you move or make any signal to the shore, we'll shoot you down like dogs."

Our second trip to the stockade alarmed the two pirates who were guarding the boats. One of them ran to the woods to tell Silver. Hunter, Joyce and I went as quickly as we could to the stockade. We threw our stores and guns over the fence, leaving Joyce there to guard them.

Then Hunter and I rowed back to the ship for another load. That load also was safely brought to the stockade and left there. This time, I returned to the ship alone.

Captain Smollett, Mr. Trelawney and I began to load the boat once more. We worked fast and desperately. At any moment, we expected Silver and his men to attack us or to attack Hunter and Joyce in the stockade. This time, the boat had to carry Captain

Smollett, Mr Trelawney, Tom Redruth and myself, four heavy men. We could not load the boat with all the stores we wished. We dropped several barrels of gun-powder and a great many guns into the sea. We had to do so. If the pirates found them, they would use them against us.

Captain Smollett was the last to leave the ship. Before climbing down into the boat, he said to the six pirates, "I'm ready to give you a last chance. Who will join us? Which of you is ready to follow his captain, and do his duty?"

The pirates made no answer. One of them, Abraham Gray, made a slight movement forward.

" Abraham Gray, I order you to follow your captain." Smollett said, taking out his watch. "You have thirty seconds to decide."

Gray made no movement.

"Come, my man, I'm risking my life and the lives of these gentlemen by staying here. You have ten seconds more."

Abraham Gray moved. The pirates tried to hold him back. He threw them off. He came running to the captain like a dog when

his master whistles.

"I'm with you, sir," he said.

Gray dropped into the boat, and the captain after him. We pushed off and began rowing in the direction of the stockade.

# 17

# THE DOCTOR TELLS OF THE SINKING OF THE BOAT

The boat was heavily overloaded. It was not built to carry five grown men, three of whom—Trelawney, Redruth and Captain Smollett—were over six feet tall. Besides, there were the stores. The water reached almost to the edge of the boat. We were all wet through before we had rowed a hundred yards.

We had to reach the stockade before the pirates did. Accordingly, we had to row fast. But, when we rowed fast, the water

poured into the boat and seemed likely to sink it.

Another danger was the current. It was carrying us towards the pirates' boats. It was some time before we got into easier water where we could keep our direction. That was a great relief to us. That was one danger over!

Then came an even greater danger. Captain Smollett saw it first.

"The cannon! Look behind you, doctor!" he cried to me.

I looked behind me. The five pirates on the Hispaniola were gathered round the cannon. In our hurry to leave the ship, we had forgotten the cannon. But the pirates had remembered! We saw them taking off its cover. Soon they were pointing the cannon straight at our boat. They were ready to fire.

"Israel was Flint's gunner," said Gray.

"Who's the best shooter among us?" Captain Smollett asked.

"Mr. Trelawney," I answered.

"Then Mr. Trelawney, will you please shoot one of those men. Hands, if you can."

Trelawney stood up carefully. We stopped rowing while he raised his gun. He fired at Hands but missed him. He hit one of the other four. We heard his cry as he fell to the deck.

At the same time, we heard shouts coming from the shore. The pirates were coming out of the woods. They were rushing towards their two boats.

"They're getting into their boats, sir," I said. I watched. Then I added, "Only one boat is away. The crew of the other are running towards the stockade. They'll be waiting for us there."

"The cannon is the chief danger," Captain Smollett said. "Mr. Trelawney, tell us when they're ready to fire and we'll stop the boat."

After a few minutes, Mr. Trelawney shouted, "Ready!"

"Hold!" cried the captain.

We stopped rowing at once. The cannon ball passed just over our heads. It fell into the sea, very near our boat. Our boat sank. Luckily, we were only thirty yards from the shore and the water was only three feet deep. No great harm was done. No lives were lost. We were all wet through; that was all. But we had lost all our stores. Besides that, three of our guns had gone down with the boat. Mine was safe and dry. I had held it over my head when the boat had sunk. The captain had done the same with his.

We had no time to grieve over our losses. We could hear the pirates in the woods near the stockade. We rushed there as fast as we could, in order to arrive there first. At every step, the shouts were nearer. We could hear the branches breaking as the pirates broke through the bushes. In a moment, they would be on us.

"Captain," I said, "Trelawney is the best shot. Let him have your gun."

Captain Smollett handed his gun to the Squire. At the same time, I handed my sword to Gray for I saw that he was unarmed.

# 18

# THE DOCTOR TELLS OF THE PIRATES' ATTACK

We reached the stockade on the south side. At the very same moment, seven of the pirates appeared at the south-west corner of the fence. Trelawney and I fired at once. Hunter and Joyce fired from inside the stockade. One of the pirates fell. The others turned and ran back to the shelter of the woods. We ran up to the man who had fallen. He was stone-dead. He had been shot through the heart.

This first success made us feel very pleased with ourselves. But not for long! Suddenly, a bullet came whistling through the air and poor Tom Redruth fell to the ground. We carried him inside the stockade.

Mr. Trelawney dropped down on his knees beside poor Tom. He kissed his hand, crying like a child. "Tom," he begged, "say that you forgive me."

"Would that be respectful, from me to you, sir?" the faithful servant said weakly. Later on, he asked me, "Am I going?"

"Tom, my man, you're going home," I told him gently.

"Will somebody say a prayer?"

Not long after, without another word, he died. Captain Smollett spread the English flag over poor Tom's body. Then he said to Mr. Trelawney, "You mustn't grieve, sir. He died while he was doing his duty."

Captain Smollett had left the Hispaniola with his pockets full of things. They held two English flags, a Bible, some rope, several pounds of tobacco, the log-book, a pen and some ink. Now, with Hunter, he climbed to the roof of the log-house and fixed a tall pole there. He tied the English flag to the pole. When he came down, he looked very pleased.

He came down just in time. A cannon ball passed over the roof and crashed into the trees nearby. Not long afterwards, a second cannon ball fell inside the stockade fence. It raised a cloud of sand but it did no damage.

"Captain Smollett, they're firing at the flag," Mr. Trelawney said. "Would it not be wiser to take it down?"

"Lower my flag, sir, Never!", the captain replied sharply.

All that evening, they were firing at us from the Hispaniola. Most of the balls went high over the roof. No damage at all was done.

"There is one good thing about this," Captain Smollett said. "The wood in front of us should be clear of our enemies. The tide is out. Our stores should be lying there, uncovered. Who will go and carry them up to the stockade?"

Gray and Hunter said that they would go. Well-armed, they crept out of the stockade and down to the beach. Then they were too late. The pirates were already busy, carrying off our stores. Long John Silver was incharge of them.

After Hunter and Gray had returned, Captain Smollett sat down to write his report on the day's happenings. That is what he wrote in his log-book:

"Alexander Smollett, captain; David Livesey, ship's doctor; Abraham Gray, ship's carpenter; John Trelawney, owner; John Hunter and Richard Joyce, owner's servants—the loyal men in the ship's company—came on shore today. They brought with them stores for ten days. At once, the English flag was put up. Thomas Redruth owner's servant, has been shot by the pirates. James Hawkins, cabin-boy..."

At that point, the captain stopped writing. He put down his pen and he looked very anxious. As the captain was writing, I was wondering about Jim. Was the poor lad alive or dead? I was beginning to fear the worst.

Then came a shout from the stockade fence, "Doctor! Captain! Hello, there!" It was Jim's voice. I ran to the door. I could hardly believe my eyes. Jim Hawkins was climbing over the fence. He was safe and sound. Thank God!

# 19

# I AM SAFE IN THE STOCKADE AND NOW CONTINUE THE STORY

The firing from the Hispaniola continued for a good hour. I ran from one hiding-place to another. Then, when the firing stopped, I ran like a hare to the stockade. My friends gave me a warm welcome.

I soon told my story. Then I began to look around me. The log-house was made of the trunks of trees. A fence, six feet high, ran all round it. The fence, too, was made of tree-trunks. Near the

door, there was a spring of pure water. There was a fire burning inside, for a cold wind was blowing. In the roof, there was a hole for the smoke to pass through. However, the wind, coming through the cracks in the walls, was blowing the smoke about the room, and into our eyes and our throats. The sand was being blown about as well. There was sand everywhere, even in our food! Besides all this, poor Tom Redruth lay dead by the wall.

We dug a grave for poor Tom in the stockade and we buried him that evening. The captain read a prayer over the grave. Then, sadly and silently, we returned to the house. We should have fallen into despair if the captain had not given us work to do. Some of us were sent out for firewood. Others had to cook. I was put on guard at the door. The captain did his best to make us feel cheerful.

From time to time, Dr. Livesey came to the door for fresh air. He stopped for a talk with me. "That fellow, Smollett, is a very brave man," he said. Then he asked me, "Jim, what do you think about Ben Gunn? Is he really mad?"

"Perhaps not quite mad, but rather mad, I think."

"Well, yes... After all, he's been living all alone for three years on this is-land. You said

that he liked cheese, didn't you?"

"Yes. He's very fond of cheese."

While we were talking, we could hear the pirates shouting and singing in their camp, about half a mile away.

"They're drunk," the doctor said, "and that will help us, Jim. Besides that, they've made their camp in a swamp. Soon all of them will be ill with malaria. There's hope for us yet, my boy."

With these cheerful words in my ears, I went to sleep. I was dead-tired. I slept like a log till sunrise. Then the sound of voices awakened me.

"It's Silver himself."

"He's carrying a white flag."

I jumped up and ran to look through a crack in the fence. Yes, there was Silver himself with another pirate. The white flag showed that they had come to make peace.

**20**

# SILVER COMES TO TALK OF PEACE

"**K**eep indoors, men!" cried Captain Smollett. "This may be a trick."

He gave us orders. "Doctor, stand on guard by the north wall. Jim, you take the east. Gray, you the west. The rest, stand by me!" Then he shouted to the two pirates, "Who goes there? Halt or we fire!"

"Captain Silver, sir. Come to make peace, sir," Silver's companion shouted.

"Captain Silver? I don't know him. Who's he?" asked Captain Smollett.

"It's me, sir," Long John answered. "The men made me captain after you had deserted the ship. We've come to make peace. Will you promise not to shoot?'

"Very well, my

man. I promise. You may come inside."

With great difficulty, Silver climbed over the fence and came towards us. I crept up behind the captain to listen. And so did the doctor and the Squire. Only Gray remained at his post.

It was hard for Silver to climb the hill to the log-house. The way was uphill and the sand was soft. At last he reached us.

"Well, here you are, my man," Captain Smollett greeted him. "You had better sit down."

"Aren't you going to ask me inside, Cap'n? It's a cold morning to sit outside on the sand."

"If you had been an honest man, you would now be sitting in your own warm galley," Captain Smollett told him.

"Well, well, Cap'n," Silver said, looking round him. "You've got a nice home here. Ah! Here's Jim. Good morning to you, Dr. Livesey, and to you, Mr. Trelawney. Why! You're all here to gether,

like a happy family...."

"If you have anything to say, my man, you had better say it quickly," Captain Smollett said sharply.

"Right you are, Cap'n. Duty is duty. Well, here it is... We want that treasure and we're going to have it. You have the map, haven't you?"

"Maybe", said Captain Smollett.

"I know you have. We want it. We must have it. Give us the map, and I'll see you safe. I'll let you choose. When we have the treasure, we'll take you on board and we'll leave you somewhere safe on shore. Or, if you'd rather, you can stay here. I'll leave you half the stores. And I'll send the first ship we meet to pick you up. I promise."

Captain Smollett stood up. "Is that all you have to say?" he asked.

"That's my last word," answered Long John. "I've made you

a generous offer. Refuse it, and you're going to be very sorry...."

"Very good," said the captain calmly. "Now, you listen to me. I'll make you an offer. Come here, one by one, unarmed, and I'll take you back to England. There you shall have a fair trial. I promise you that. If you won't do that, I'll see you all dead before I leave this island. You're in a nasty corner, Silver. You all are. You can't find the treasure because we have the map. You can't sail the ship. There's no one of you able to, without me. You can't fight us and win. Why, five of you weren't able to hold Gray back. These are the last good words you'll ever get from me, Silver. The next time we meet, I'll shoot you down like a dog. And now, off with you, my man! Double-quick!"

Silver was white with fury. He moved to get up. "Who's going to help me up?" he asked.

Nobody moved. Silver crawled over the sand to the wall. There he lifted himself on his crutch. He shook his fist at us. "Before an hour's gone, I'll break your house to bits," he shouted. "I'll tear your hearts out— with my own hands! I will ! I swear I will !" Then he made his slow way to the fence. His companion helped him to climb over. They both disappeared among the trees.

# 21

# THE PIRATES ATTACK THE LOG-HOUSE

Captain Smollett stood there, watching Silver till he was out of sight. Then he turned round and found that only Gray was at his post. Never before had I seen the captain so angry.

"To your posts!" he roared. "Gray, you've done your duty like a true seaman. Mr Trelawney. I'm surprised at you, sir. Doctor, I thought that you had been a soldier...."

We went back to our posts with red faces. We began loading the guns. The captain watched us for a time in silence. Then he said, "My lads, before the hour's out, they'll attack us. As you know, their numbers are greater than ours. On the other hand, we're fighting in shelter. If every one of you does his duty, we can beat them. I'm certain of that."

We got ready for the attack. The guns and the gun-powder were all laid ready. The fire was put out so that the smoke would not hurt our eyes. I prepared the breakfast. We ate it in a hurry. Then we drank a glass of rum each.

Captain Smollett gave us our orders. "Doctor, your post is by the door. Hunter, you'll defend the east wall. Joyce, the west. Mr. Trelawney and Gray, the north wall—that's where the greatest danger is. Hawkins, you'll help me to load the guns."

By this time, the sun was high in the sky. It was growing hot. We took off our coats and opened our shirts at the neck. We waited anxiously.

An hour passed. Then came the first sign of the pirates.

"If I see anyone, shall I fire?" Joyce asked politely.

"I told you so!" cried the captain.

"Thank you, sir." Joyce said and then fired.

From all sides, the pirates began shooting. Several shots struck the log-house but they did no damage. The smoke cleared away and the shooting stopped. Silence fell on the stockade and the woods nearby. There was nothing to show that our enemies were there.

"Did you hit your man?" the captain asked Joyce.

"No, sir. I believe not, sir."

"Better luck next time! Load his gun, Hawkins." Then Captain Smollett asked, "How many do you think there are on your side, doctor?"

"Three."

"How many on yours, Mr. Trelawney?"

"Seven."

"Eight or nine," Gray said.

Hardly had he finished speaking when the pirates ran out from the woods to the north of us. They made for the stockade fence. Like monkeys, they climbed over it. Mr. Trelawney and Gray kept on firing. Three pirates fell. Two lay there, quite still. One got up and ran away. Four of them were left and they came rushing towards us. Job Anderson was at their head.

A pirate suddenly appeared at Hunter's loop-hole. He seized Hunter's gun and stuck Hunter on the head with it. Poor Hunter fell senseless to the ground. Another pirate rushed at the doctor by the door. The log-house was filled with smoke, cries, and the sounds of pistol shots.

"Out, lads! Fight them in the open! Swords!" shouted the captain.

I seized a sword and rushed out of doors. I found myself face to face with Job Anderson. He roared and raised his sword to strike. I jumped to one side. My foot slipped in the soft sand and I went rolling down the hill. Gray was close behind me. With a single stroke, he cut Anderson down. Now, of the four pirates who had climbed into the stockade, only one was unwounded. He ran away.

"Back to the house!" came the doctor's shout. "Fire from there!'

We ran back to the log-house. At any moment we expected the firing to begin again. For a moment, the victory was ours, but we had paid a heavy price for it. Hunter lay on the floor, senseless from that blow on the head. Joyce had been shot dead at his post. The captain had been wounded.

"Have they run?" Captain Smollett asked weakly.

"All those who could," answered the doctor. "Five of them will never run again."

"Five!" said the captain, "That's better. They've lost five men and we only three. Now there are four of us against nine of them. When we started, we were seven against nineteen. We'll beat them yet."

# 22

# MY SEA ADVENTURE

L uckily, the pirates did not attack us again that day. Poor Hunter died that afternoon. Captain Smollett's wound was serious but not dangerous. He would not be able to use his right arm for a month.

After dinner, Mr. Trelawney and the doctor sat talking for a time at the captain's side. Then the doctor stood up. He took his hat and his pistols and he put the map into his pocket. Then he left the log-house. He climbed over the fence and went off through the trees. Gray and I watched him go.

"Has the doctor gone mad?" Gray asked me.

"I think he has gone off to talk with Ben Gunn." I was right but I did not know that till sometime afterwards.

Inside the log-house, the heat was suffocating. I envied the doctor, walking in the shady wood. And then I felt that I must go too. If I had asked permission, they would have refused it. I decided not to ask. I filled my pockets with biscuits and took a couple of pistols. Then, when nobody was looking, I crept out. In a few seconds, I was over the fence and away.

My plan was to go to the White Rock to look for Ben Gunn's boat. I made my way through the wood and came out on the shore. It was now almost evening. The air was fresh and the sea was blue. I began to enjoy myself. I saw the Hispaniola lying at anchor on the calm sea. I hid in some bushes and watched her.

A boat lay near the ship. I could see Silver in it. He was talking to two men who were on board. Then Silver's boat returned to the shore. The two men went below.

It was now sunset. A mist was spreading and it was growing dark. I had no time to lose. I had to find Ben Gunn's boat before nightfall. I crept through the bushes towards the White Rock.

Yes, the boat was there. But what a boat! It was made of goatskins, stretched over a wooden frame. It looked too small to hold me. I sat down, ate my supper, and made a plan. This was my plan: as soon as it was dark, I would row out to the Hispaniola. I could cut her anchor-rope. Then the wind and the current would carry her away. After their defeat, I thought, the pirates would be eager to sail away. I would

prevent them from doing that.

It was a perfect night for my plan. There was a thick mist and no moon. Ben Gunn's boat was very light. I put it on my shoulder and made for the sea. The darkness was complete except for the light from the pirates' fire. There they sat, drinking, shouting and singing. Seawards, a fainter light showed from the Hispaniola.

The tide was out. I walked a long way over the wet sand. When I reached the sea, I set the boat in the water. I got in. The boat was safe, but it was very hard to control. It went round and round if I stopped rowing. And, unless I rowed hard, it went sideways, like a crab. I should never have reached the Hispaniola if the current had not carried me there.

At last I reached the ship. I easily found the rope that held her. I took out my knife, opened it with my teeth and cut almost through the rope. I then rested a moment.

It was then that I heard loud voice from the cabin. Two men were shouting and quarrelling. One of them was Israel Hands who had been Flint's gunner. The other was the pirate they called "Redbeard" because of the thick red hair on his chin. Both men were drunk. Even as I lay there resting, the cabin window was thrown

open. An empty bottle passed dangerously near my head!

Looking towards the shore, I could see the pirates' camp-fire. I could even hear them singing:

"Fifteen men on the dead man's chest—

Yo—ho—ho, and a bottle of rum!

Drink and the devil had done for the rest—

Yo—ho—ho, and a bottle of rum!"

I began to think of the old Benbow, my mother, and home. But I had no time for memories. The current brought my boat nearer the ship. I took my knife and this time cut the rope quite through. The Hispaniola was now free of her anchor. She was now at the mercy of the current and the wind. She was still very near me. I stood up in my boat and looked through the cabin window. Hands and Red-beard were fighting, each with a hand upon the other's throat!

I dropped into my boat. Not a minute too soon! A strong current caught my boat and the Hispaniola. At a fearful speed, it carried us towards the open sea.

There, for certain, we should meet with rough waves. Death seemed very near me. I lay down in my little boat, waiting for the end. I prayed. At last, in spite of the danger, I fell asleep. I dreamt of my mother and the old Benbow Inn.

# 23

# I BOARD THE HISPANIOLA

It was broad day when I awoke. I found myself alive in my little boat. I was off the south-west end of Treasure Island and only a quarter of mile off the shore.

I began to row towards the land. However, I soon stopped rowing for I saw that there was no landing-place there. The rocks were too sharp and the waves too rough. I lay down again in the boat and let the current carry me northwards. I hoped to be able to reach the Cape of the Woods where I could make a safe landing.

By this time, I was very thirsty. The sun shone down with a fierce heat. I felt that I should soon die of thirst. I sat up. The Cape of the

Woods was in sight. Among those green trees, I should surely find water. Then I should drink. Ah! How I should drink? At that moment, I would have given all my share of the treasure for a glass of water!

The current carried me past the Cape of the Woods and on to the next bay. There I saw something that made me forget my thirst. I saw the Hispaniola, not half a mile away!

I stared. I could not believe my eyes. The Hispaniola was sailing in a strange way. She was sailing north, south, east and west! It was clear to me that nobody was steering her. Where were Israel Hands and his companion Red-beard? Were they drunk or dead? Had they left the ship?

I decided to get on board if I could. I needed water badly. I was anxious to see what had happened. If I were lucky, I might be able to return the ship to Captain Smollett.....

Thinking thus, I rowed towards the ship. Soon I was very near. Nobody appeared on deck. Was there anybody on the ship? Was it a trick? Were they hiding? If Hands and his companion were in the cabin, I could lock them in. Then I could do what I liked with the ship.........

I was about a hundred yards away when a wind sprang up. It carried the ship away from me. I followed her. I was beside her. A wave lifted me high in the air. I seized the nearest rope. The wave carried my boat away. And there was I, hanging from the rope at the side of the ship. I had to go on board now. Quickly I climbed the rope, hand over hand. Then I fell head-first on to the deck.

# 24

# ON BOARD THE HISPANIOLA

The two pirates were still on the ship. Red-beard lay on his back on the deck. His arms were spread out and his mouth was open wide. He was dead. Israel Hands lay beside him, with his face as white as a sheet. Was he alive or dead? As I was wondering, Hands moved and gave a groan. He opened his eyes and saw me. "Here I am, Mr. Hands," I said to him.

"Rum," he gasped. "Rum, quick!"

He looked as if he were dying. I ran below to fetch him some rum. The cabin was a terrible sight. All the cupboards had been broken open. Empty bottles

were lying everywhere. The floor was covered with dirt and mud. I hurried to the store. The barrels of rum were all empty. I found a bottle of brandy and took that. For myself, I took some biscuits, cheese, and dried fruits. Then I hurried back to Hands on the deck. On the way, I went to the water barrel and had a good drink. Ah! How good that water tasted. I hurried towards Hands and gave him some brandy.

"Ah!" he said, "I needed that."

I sat down not very far from him and began eating hungrily.

"Are you badly hurt?" I asked.

He growled.

"Well," I said, "I've come on board to take charge of the ship. I'm the captain now—till further orders."

Hands gave me a black look but he did not speak. He was beginning to look a little better. He now had some colour in his cheeks.

I pointed to the pirates' black flag. "I can't have that flag fly-

ing over the ship," I told him. I got up, pulled the flag down and threw it overboard. "God save the King!" I cried, waving my cap.

His eyes never left me. "Cap'n Hawkins," he said, "you and me should have a little talk."

"Talk on, Mr. Hands," I said, and went on with my meal.

"He's dead," Hands said, with a look at his companion. "And who's going to sail this ship now? You can't unless I tell you how. I'll tell you how if you give me food and drink and something to put round this wound in my leg. What do you say to that?"

"Very well, it's a bargain. But I'm not going back to the old place. I mean to sail her to North Bay."

"It's all the same to me," Hands said.

I went below and took from my chest a soft, silk handkerchief of my mother's. I helped Hands to bandage his leg with this. He drank some more of the brandy and also ate some bread and cheese. He began to look his old self again.

I was feeling very pleased with myself. I had good hopes of bringing the ship into North Bay. If I did that, my friends would forgive my leaving the log-house without permission. I now had plenty of water to drink and plenty of food to eat. The weather was fine. And here was I, Jim Hawkins, Captain of the good ship Hispaniola! However, there was one thing that troubled me all the time. Hands kept his eyes on me. They never left me. They watched every movement that I made. And in his eyes, I read treachery. Yes, he was waiting for a chance to attack me and to kill me. I was sure of that.

# 25

# ISRAEL HANDS ATTEMPTS TO KILL ME AND DIES IN THE ATTEMPT

Hands told me how to steer the ship and we sailed smoothly towards North Bay. Hands was watching me all the time. Suddenly, he said, "Jim, will you go below and fetch me a bottle of wine. This brandy is too strong. It's giving me a headache."

I did not believe him. The pirates liked rum and brandy much better than wine. Wine was not strong enough for them. It was clear that Hands wanted me to leave the deck. I did not know why, but I was determined to find out.

"A bottle of wine?" I said to him.

"That's a good idea. Wine is better for you than brandy. Would you like red or white wine?"

"I don't mind. But I want it strong, and plenty of it."

"I'll bring you red, Mr. Hands. But I'll have to look for it. It may take some time to find a bottle."

I ran off noisily. Then, when I was below, I took off my shoes and crept like a mouse to the other stairs. Up I crept and put my head out. I could see what Hands was doing. He was creeping along the deck towards a coil of rope. Now and then, he gave a groan because of the pain in his leg. But he moved swiftly. He put his hand inside the coil and drew out a knife. He hid this inside his coat and crept back to his place.

I had seen enough. Hands had a knife on him and he could move about. He was dangerous and he was ready to kill me. That was certain. However, for the moment, I was safe.  Hands needed me for the beaching of the ship. When the ship was on the beach, he would attack me. Then I crept back to the cabin and put on my shoes. I found a bottle of red wine and went up on deck with it.

Hands was lying there with his eyes shut. He was groaning. "Jim," he said weakly, "I'm dying." He drank some wine and then lay still for some time.

We were now only two miles off North Bay. Till now, steering the ship had been easy. Now it began to be difficult. The entrance to the bay was narrow and dangerous. Hands certainly knew his job. The orders he gave me were excellent. I carried them out quickly and well. The tide was going out and very soon we should be able to beach the ship. I steered her through the shallow water to the sandy shore. In a few minutes, we should touch land.

I was leaning over the side to look at the depth of the water. Suddenly, something made me look up. Hands was coming towards me, with his knife in his hand!

He sprang at me like a wild beast. With a cry of terror, I jumped to one side. Hands' blow missed me and he fell to the ground. Before he could get up, I had run to the far end of the deck. Hands came after me. I took out my pistol and pointed it straight at him. But the powder was wet and the pistol did not fire. Hands was coming nearer. Although he was wounded, he was moving fast. I had another pistol in my pocket. There was no time for me to load that. Hands was very near. I jumped to one side and ran for wards. Again he came after me.

Suddenly, the Hispaniola struck the beach and went over to one side. Hands and I were thrown to the side. Red-beard came slipping after us. My head came against Hands' foot with a terrible "crack", but I sprang up before Hands could.

Hand over hand, I climbed up the mast. Like a monkey I climbed. My quickness saved me. Hands threw his knife at me. It struck the mast not six inches below me. I looked down. There he stood, undecided what to do next.

Sitting high up the mast, I loaded my pistols with dry powder.

Slowly and painfully, Hands began to climb up after me. He was holding his knife between his teeth. With a loaded pistol in each hand, I shouted to him, "One more step, Mr. Hands, and I'll fire." I added, with a laugh, "Dead men don't bite, you know!"

Hands stopped. He took his knife from his mouth in order to answer me. "Jim," he said, "If the ship hadn't rolled, I should have got you. I never have any luck. You've won, my lad. You've won."

These words were as sweet as honey to me. The next moment, he raised his right hand. His knife shot through the air like an arrow. I felt a sudden blow and then a sharp pain. I was pinned to the mast by his knife in my shoulder!

In the pain and surprise of the moment, both my pistols went off. Both of them dropped from my hands and into the sea. At the same time, Hands gave a low cry and fell head-first into the water.

# 26

# I LEAVE THE HISPANIOLA AND AM CAUGHT BY THE ENEMY

The Hispaniola lay on her side. From my seat on the mast, I could see straight down to the bottom of the sea. Hands' body rose once and then it sank for ever. He was shot and drowned. His body lay there on the clean sand at the side of the ship. Three or four fishes went swimming over it.

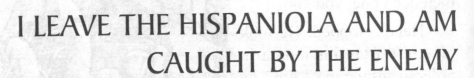

I began to feel sick and faint. My shoulder was aching badly. I could feel the hot blood running down my back and my chest. For a moment, I thought that I was going to faint. I shut my eyes and sat there quietly. Slowly I became calm again. Then I tried to pull the knife out of my shoulder. It was impossible. My body began to shake with fear and pain. That shaking saved me. It tore my skin away from the knife. The blood flowed faster. I did not mind that. I was free. After that, it was easy to tear my coat and shirt free.

I climbed down to the deck. I went below to bandage my shoulder. The wound was bleeding a lot but it was not deep or dangerous. I went back to the deck. The sun was setting. The bay was already in deep shadow. The cold evening breeze had begun to blow. It was time for me to be going.

Before I left the ship, I went back to the body of Hands' companion, Red-beard. I dragged it to the edge of the deck and pushed it into the sea. I looked down. There the two bodies lay, side by side, with the quick fishes swimming over them.

I climbed down a rope and dropped into the sea. The water was shallow and hardly reached my waist. The sand was firm and I soon reached the shore. Then I began hurrying in the direction of the log-house. I was eager to see my friends again and to tell them what had happened. Perhaps they would be angry with me for leaving them secretly. But they would forgive me because I had brought them the Hispaniola.

It was a hard journey. I kept falling over bushes and rolling into holes. When the moon rose, however, I could go faster. I even ran.

At last, the stockade came into sight. The fence on the

western side shown silver in the moonlight. The log-house itself lay in a black shadow. On the other side of the house, a red light came from a dying fire. Nobody was moving. Not a sound came from the place.

Suddenly, I felt afraid. Why was there nobody on guard? Why was that big fire outside? Captain Smollett had always forbidden a fire outside. Something was wrong. Something had happened during my absence. Well, I had better go and see!

Very quietly, I made my way to the door of the log-house. I stood there, listening. I heard the heavy breathing of men asleep. It was a welcome sound. Surely it meant that my friends were sleeping. A sudden idea came to me. I would walk in and lie down in my usual place. In the morning, when they woke up, they would find me there. What a surprise for them! I laughed to myself as I pictured their faces.

I walked inside very quietly. My foot touched something soft. It was somebody's leg. The sleeper turned over but he did not wake up. I crept on. Suddenly the silence was broken. A shrill voice rang out, "Ay! Ay! Sir. Ship ahoy! Seaward ho!" It was Silver's parrot, Captain Flint. He was on guard. And a good guard he was. His cries woke everybody up. Silver shouted, "Who goes there?"

I turned to run away, but from all sides strong arms held me fast.

"Bring a light, Dickl!" cried Silver.

Dick ran outside and was soon back with a blazing torch.

# 27

# IN THE HANDS OF THE PIRATES

The blazing torch showed me that my fears were true. The pirates held the log-house and the stores. I looked round me. I could see no prisoners. Had they killed all my friends? Oh! Why had I not been there to die with them.

There were six of the pirates left. One had a blood-stained bandage round his head. The other looked drunk and ill. Silver himself looked pale and stern. His clothes were torn and muddy. With the parrot on his shoulder, he stood there, looking at me.

"We'll," he cried, "here's Jim Hawkins come to see us. This is a nice surprise, my lad, and you're very welcome. I always said that you were a bright lad but I never expected this."

I said nothing. I stood there with my back to the wall. I looked Silver straight in the face. There was black despair in my heart but I tried to look brave. Silver sat down on the rum barrel and began smoking. "Now, Jim," he said, "I've always liked you. I've always wanted you to join us. Now you just have to. You can't go back to your friends. They won't take you back, Jim. They say that you've deserted them. You'll have to join us."

How glad I was to learn that my friends were alive! I did not believe that they would not have me back. Silver was a liar.

"Now, Jim, think it over, lad. You're free to say yes or no, as you like. Think it over carefully! You've plenty of time. We're glad to have you with us. We're enjoying your company."

"Very well," I answered, "I'll think it over. But first, you must tell me why you're here and where my friends are."

"Right you are, mate," Silver said, still speaking very pleasantly. "I'll tell you. Yesterday morning, Dr. Livesey came up to us with the white flag. `Ship's gone,' he told us. We looked out. By thunder! the old ship had gone! `Well,' said the doctor, `you and I, Silver, will have a little talk.' And so we did. In the end, we agreed to take the log-house and the stores. In return, we let them march off—I don't know where. `How many of you are there?' I asked him. `Four,' he said, `myself, Mr. Trelawney, Captain Smollett and Gray.' Then I asked him, `What about young Hawkins?' And he said, `We don't know where he is. And we don't care. We're tired of him and his tricks.' So you see how it is, Jim, my lad."

"Is that all you have to tell me?" I asked.

"That's all."

"Then I'll tell you something," I said breathlessly. "You're in a tight corner, Silver. Your ship's gone. You haven't got the map and so you can't find the trea- s u r e . You've lost more than half of your men. And the six here look sick. Yes, you're in a

tight corner. And who put you there, Silver? I! I, Jim Hawkins! I put you there! I overheard your plans that last night at sea. I was in the apple barrel while you were talking to Hands and Dick. At once I told my friends every word that you had said." I stopped for breath. I was shaking like a leaf from fear and from fury. Then I went on. "As for the ship. Who cut her loose? I did. I cut her loose. And I've left her where you'll never find her. Kill me, if you like. Kill me, I say! I'd rather die than join you."

I had to stop, for I was quite out of breath. To my surprise, nobody moved. They stood there like sheep. Silver was looking at me in a friendly way, I thought. Then Tom Morgan, who had seen me in the Spy-glass Inn, shouted,

"He knew Black Dog."

"He knew Billy Bones as well," said Silver. "It was he who took his map."

Morgan sprang up with a knife in his hand. His arm was raised to strike me.

"Stop that!" shouted Silver. "Get away from that lad, Tom

Morgan! If you want to fight, come and fight me! I'm the captain here, remember."

Morgan obeyed unwillingly. His companions were on his side. They were all against Silver. They gathered together and began whispering.

"Listen!" cried Silver. "This lad is worth a hundred of you rats. By thunder! I'll tear the heart out of any man who touches him."

The men went on whispering among themselves, with many black looks at Silver and myself.

"You seem to have a lot to say," Silver told them. "Speak up!"

"We're going outside to choose a new captain. We're sick and tired of you, Silver. You've fooled us all the time."

They all went outside, leaving Silver and me in the log-house alone. My heart was beating very fast. Silver had saved me. Would he be able to save me when the men came back?

"Listen, Jim," Silver whispered. "They're going to throw me off. I'll save you if I can. But, remember, you must save me when the time comes."

"You mean that—that all is lost."

"I do. The ship's gone and we can't get away. In the end, we'll be caught and then we'll be hanged. But you'll speak for me, won't you, Jim? You won't forget that I saved you........."

"I'll do what I can," I promised him.

He drew some rum from the barrel and drank it eagerly. "Would you like a drop, mate?" he asked me. I refused, and he went on talking. "I need a drop of rum, Jim. There's trouble ahead. But remember that I'm on your side, lad." Then, suddenly, he asked me, "Why did the doctor give me that map?"

"Did he give you the map?" I asked in great astonishment.

"Yes, and I don't know why." He took another drink of rum. " I know one thing, mate," he said. "There's trouble ahead for you and me.

# 28

# THE BLACK SPOT ONCE MORE

I went to a loop-hole and looked out. The five pirates were gathered round the dying fire. One of them was on his knees, with a knife in one hand and a book in the other. The others were bending over him, watching him closely. The kneeling man stood up. Then they came slowly back to the log-house.

"Here they are," I said.

"Let them come, mate. I'm ready for them," Silver said cheerfully.

The door opened slowly. One of the pirates was pushed forward. He held his closed right hand in front of him.

"Come on, lad," cried Silver. "I won't eat you. Hand it over. I know the rules, I do. I won't hurt you."

The pirate then put something into Silver's hand. Long John looked at it.

"The black Spot! Ha! I thought so. Where did you find the paper?" He looked at it closely. "Why! you've cut it out of a Bible. That'll bring bad luck, for certain."

"I told you so," Tom Morgan said to the others. "It'll bring us bad luck."

"What fool has cut a Bible?" asked Silver.

"It was Dick."

"He'll hang for certain. He'll.........."

He was interrupted. "Stop this talk!" George Merry cried. "Let's go on with the business. We've given you the Black Spot, according to the rules. Turn it over and see what's on the back. Then you can talk, if you want to."

"Thank you, George. You always had a head for business. And you know the rules by heart, I see. Well, let's see what's on the back."

Silver turned the paper over. "Thrown off" he read. Then he said, "The handwriting's very good. Is it yours, George? You're quite a leader now, aren't you? Maybe, you're thinking of being captain......."

"We're finished with you, Silver," George Merry said. "You've fooled us long enough. Now, by the rules, you must vote, with us, for a new captain."

"I thought you knew the rules, George," Silver said, with a laugh. "If you don't, I do. I'm still your captain till you've made your complaints and I've replied. Till then, your Black Spot is worthless."

"Here you are then," George Merry said. "Here are our complaints. First, everything has gone wrong on this voyage, thanks to you. Secondly, you've let the enemy get out of here—and for nothing. Thirdly, you wouldn't let us attack them while they were leaving. Fourthly, there's this boy here......."

"Is that all?" asked Silver.

"It's enough. We shall all hang, thanks to you......"

"Well now, I'll answer your points. First, I've let everything go wrong on this voyage, have I? Why! It was you, George Merry, you, and Hands, and Anderson who crossed me all the time. If you

had listened to me, we should all have been safely on the ship, with the treasure. But you wouldn't wait—as I told you to."

Silver paused. The men's faces showed that they knew Silver was right. Then Silver went on. "Now, your second point. Why did I let them leave here—for nothing—so you say. Well, I'll answer that in a minute. You ask why I didn't shoot them on their way out. You fool! Don't you understand that we need a doctor. You above all, George Merry, with your eyes yellow with malaria. And you, John, with that wound in your head. As for the boy here—he'll be a useful prisoner. Either they'll do what we want or we'll kill him. Haven't you thought of that? Fools! What sort of pirates are you?"

Silver stopped. The men were now listening quietly to him. He was winning them back to his side. "Now, George Merry, your second point," he continued. "You want to know why I let them leave here. Well, I'll tell you. I made a bargain with them. If I hadn't , you'd have died of hunger. Why did I let them go? That's the reason. And the best reason of all, is this......."

Silver flung the map on the floor in front of them.

The pirates could hardly believe their eyes. They sprang on it, like cats on a mouse. They passed it from hand to hand. From their cries, you would have thought that they were handling the treasure itself!

Then George Merry spoke up. "All right, Silver, but I want to know this.............How are we going to get away with the treasure when we have no ship? Tell me that!"

"George Merry!" cried Silver, "one more word from you, and I'll cut you down like a dog. It was you who lost the ship for us. You should be telling us how to get away. I've had enough. I've had more than enough. I've finished with the lot of you. Elect your new captain......."

"Silver!" they all shouted. "Barbecue for ever! Barbecue's our Cap'n!"

Long John Silver smiled. "Well, George," he said, "it seems that you'll have to wait a little longer for my place. It's lucky that I'm a forgiving man." He looked down at the Black Spot. "Well, mates, what are we going to do with this? It's no use at all now, is it?" He handed it to me, saying, "Here, Jim, you take it. It'll be a nice souvenir.

The pirates began drinking. I was tired to death. I lay down and fell asleep at once.

# 29

# I AM A PRISONER

I was awakened by a shout from the edge of the wood.

"Ahoy there! Here's the doctor."

It was Dr. Livesey, who had come to visit his patients.

I was very happy to hear his voice again. But I also felt ashamed. I had run away from the log-house. What would the doctor think when he found me among the pirates?

Silver went outside to meet him. I heard him shouting cheerfully, "Good morning to you, sir." Then, as the doctor came nearer, I heard him say, "We've a nice surprise for you this morning, doctor. We've a little stranger here. A new lodger, sir. Ha! Ha! He's looking well. Slept like a log, he did."

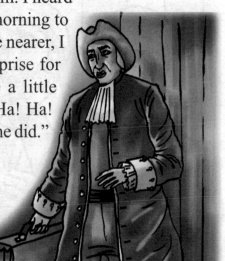

"Not Jim?"

"Jim it is."

I heard the doctor stop. Then he said, "Well, well, duty first and pleasure afterwards. I'll see my patients first." Dr. Livesey came in. He nodded to me. Then he went to examine his patients. He worked quietly as if he were visiting an English family in a quiet English village. He showed no fear at all. The men behaved as if he were still the ship's doctor and they were the loyal crew.

"Dick isn't feeling well, sir," said one of the pirates.

"That's because he cut his Bible," said Morgan. "I told him he'd have bad luck."

The doctor examined Dick. "It's malaria," he said. "You'll all get it. It's your own fault for camping in a swamp. What did you expect?"

When the doctor had finished his work, he said to Silver, "I'd like a word with that boy before I go."

"No!" shouted Morgan.

"Silence!" roared Silver, and he looked fiercely round at his men. Then he turned to the doctor. "We're grateful to you, doctor, for your help. We trust you and we trust the boy. Hawkins, will you give me your word of honour not to run away?"

I promised at once.

"Now, doctor, will you step outside the stockade? I'll bring the boy down to you. You can talk to each other through the fence."

When the doctor had gone, there was a lot of angry talking among the men. They said that Silver was too friendly towards the doctor. I heard Morgan say, "He's fooling us again."

"By thunder I shall be friendly—till the time comes," Silver told them angrily. Then he left the house with me, with his hand on my shoulder.

When we reached the fence, Silver said very softly to the doctor, "You won't forget, sir, that I saved this boy's life. They threw me off for that, they did. I'm in a nasty corner at the moment, sir." He walked a short distance away from us and sat down to wait till we had finished our talk.

"So, Jim," said Dr. Livesey sadly, "here you are, a prisoner. I'm not blaming you, Jim. But it was wrong to run away when Captain Smollett was wounded. If he had been well, you wouldn't have dared. It was cowardly of you......."

His words made me cry. "I know I've done wrong," I told him. "I know it. I deserve to die. And they're going to kill me, sir. If Silver hadn't stopped them, I should have been dead already. I'm not afraid of dying. But if they torture me, I may........""Dr. Livesey interrupted me. "Jim, that mustn't happen. Jump over the fence, Jim! Then we'll run........."

"I can't. I've given my word of honour."

"Never mind that! Jump! Jump!"

"No, sir. But let me finish what I was saying. If they torture me, I may say where I've left the ship. I got the ship, sir. She's lying in North Bay."

"You got the ship!" the doctor exclaimed.

I told Dr. Livesey what had happened. When I had finished, he said, "There is a kind of fate in this. At every step, you save our lives, Jim. You found out Silver's plan. You found Ben Gunn. That was the best deed of all. And, speaking of Ben Gunn......." the doctor stopped and then shouted, "Silver!"

Silver came up to us. "I'll give you a piece of advice," the doctor said to him. "Don't hurry after that treasure!"

"Why, sir!" Silver said, "I've got to go after it at once. The men are restless. They'll kill the boy and me too if we don't hurry after it."

"Well then, be ready for trouble when you find the place."

Silver was clearly puzzled. "You must tell me more than that," he said. "I can't understand why you left the stockade. I don't know why you gave me the map. If you don't tell me more, I'll do nothing more for you."

"Silver, I can't tell you any more. I've no right to do so. But you've been good to this boy. And so I'll make you a promise. If we get away from this island, I'll do my best to save you."

Silver's face shone. "You're a real gentleman, sir," he said.

"Another thing," went on the doctor. "When you go after the treasure, keep the boy close to you. When you need help, shout for us. I won't forget what you've done for Jim. We're grateful to you for that, Silver." The doctor finished speaking and walked quickly away towards the wood.

# 30

# THE TREASURE HUNT

"Jim," Silver said, on our way back to the log-house, "there's a lot I don't understand. But you stick by me?, mate, and I'll stick by you. We'll save our necks in spite of fate and fortune."

We sat round the fire to have our breakfast. Silver sat with his parrot on his shoulder. "Ay! Ay! Sir," the parrot screamed. "Ay! Ay! Sir. Ship ahoy! Seaward ho!" Over and over again, the parrot repeated these words. Silver was talking to the men while he was eating. "Ay, mates, it's lucky for you that you have Barbecue to think for you. I got what I wanted from the doctor. He told me

that they have the ship. Well, we'll get the treasure, lads. Then we'll find the ship. Oh, yes! we'll find it. We've got the boats, remember! Then we'll sail away."

Hearing this, the men were in better spirits. My spirits, however, were low. How could I trust Silver? If he got the treasure and the ship, he would kill me and my friends. That was certain. Even if Silver were ready to help me, we were two against five. The doctor had told us to expect trouble.......Such thoughts left me with little appetite for my breakfast.

Silver's next words added to my fears. "As for this boy—he's had his last talk with his friends. We'll keep him with us for a time. He may still be useful. But, when we've got the treasure and the ship, then, mates, he'll have his reward. And so will his friends.........."

After breakfast, we set out to hunt for the treasure. All the men carried spades. All of them but I, were armed. I was tied to Silver by a long rope. I had to follow him like a dog. We made our way to the beach and got into the two boats.

As we rowed, there was a lot of talk about the map. The writing on the back was a great puzzle to the pirates. it said:

"Tall tree, Spy-glass shoulder, bearing a point to the N. of N.N.E.

Skeleton Island E.S.E. and by E.

Ten feet."

One thing alone was clear to all. A tall tree on Spy-glass Hill was the aim. But which tall tree? The top of Spy-glass Hill was covered with tall trees.

We landed and began to climb Spy-glass Hill. Long before we reached the top, each pirate had picked out a different tree as the "tall tree".

We were near the top when a shout came from a pirate to the left of us. It was a shout of terror. The others ran towards their companion. The skeleton of a man lay at the foot of a tall tree. Grass was growing over it. Some rags of clothing were still left on the bones. George Merry, bolder than the rest, touched the rags.

"He was a seaman," he said. "This was good sea-cloth."

"Look how he's lying," cried Silver. "It's not natural. A dead man should not be lying like that."

The dead man lay perfectly straight. His feet pointed in one direction. His hands, raised above his head, pointed in the opposite direction.

"I have an idea," Silver cried in some excitement. He took his compass out of his pocket and handed it to Dick. "Here's the compass, Dick. There's the top of Skeleton Island. Take a bearing along the line of these bones."

Dick took the bearing. The body pointed straight towards Skeleton Island, and the compass showed E.S.E. and by E.

"I thought so," Silver said, "Straight up there is our line for the treasure. By thunder! it makes me cold inside to think of Flint. After he had killed the six men with him, he dragged this one here.

He laid him down by the compass. This fellow is Flint's pointer. Flint's pointer!" Silver stopped and looked at the bones for a time. Then he continued. "Long bones........ and fair hair. I think it was Allardyce. Do you remember Allardyce, Tom Morgan?

"Oh, yes! I remember him. He owed me money. And he took my knife on shore with him." A thought struck him. "Where's his knife? It ought to be here."

"So it ought," said Silver. "Have a look round, George!"

"There's no knife here," George Merry said, after looking around.

"Strange," Silver said. He looked thoughtful. "There's something that isn't natural here." He paused and added, "If Flint were here now, you and I would be in a nasty corner."

"Flint's dead," said Morgan, "I saw him dead."

"I saw him die," another pirate said. "A terrible death it was. He was shouting for rum and singing and cursing till the end."

"If ever a man's ghost walked, his would," Morgan said.

"Stop this talk!" cried Silver. "Flint's dead and we're here to find his treasure. Come on, mates!"

We went on. The pirates walked close together now. They spoke in low voices. At any moment, they expected to meet the ghost of Captain Flint!

# 31

# THE GHOST OF CAPTAIN FLINT

After a slow and silent climb, we reached the top of Spyglass Hill. We sat down for a moment to rest. The pirates were not tired but they were frightened. Silver took out his compass. He told us, "There are three tall trees in the right line from Skeleton Island. The treasure won't be hard to find now, mates. I'd like my dinner before we go any farther.

"I'm not hungry. My appetite's gone," Morgan said.

"Listen! Flint's dead and buried. I tell you," cried Silver.

"He was an ugly devil," another pirate

said. "Blue in the face, he was."

"The rum made him like that," George Merry explained.

All of them spoke in low voices, as if Captain Flint might hear them. They were almost whispering. The woods around us were silent.

Suddenly, from the trees in front of us, a high, shaking voice began singing:

"Fifteen men on the dead man's chest—

　　Yo—ho—ho, and a bottle of rum!

Drink and the devil had done for the rest—

　　Yo—ho—ho, and a bottle of rum!"

The pirates were terrified. Their faces turned white. Several jumped up. Morgan rolled on the ground.

"It's Flint!" screamed George Merry.

The singing stopped as suddenly as it had begun.

Silver's face was grey. "Come, lads," he said, "this won't do. Somebody is playing a trick on us."

Then from the trees, the same high, shaking voice called out. "Darby M'Graw! Darby M'Graw! Fetch me the rum, Darby!"

The pirates seemed to turn to stone. Their eyes showed their terror.

"Those were Flint's last words," Morgan whispered in horror. "His last words before he died."

Silver fought bravely against his fear. "I'm here to get that treasure," he said. "And

I won't be beaten by man or devil. No! I tell you. I never feared Flint when he was alive. I won't fear him now he's dead. Come on, mates! There's seven hundred thousand pounds lying a quarter of mile away. Come with me and get it."

"We'll never get it. His ghost is walking........"

"Ghost! That was no ghost! A ghost has no shadow and his voice has no echo. Didn't you hear the echo just now?"

This strange reasoning seemed to give some strength back to the pirates.

"You're right, John," cried George Merry. "That voice ......... It wasn't like Flint's voice. It was like........"

"By thunder! Ben Gunn's!"

"So it was," cried Morgan, "It was Ben Gunn. Nobody minds Ben Gunn. Dead or alive, who minds Ben Gunn?"

The pirates were cheerful again. They finished their dinner, took up their spades and went on again. George Merry led the way. He held Silver's compass in his hand to keep them all on the right line.

They soon reached the first of the tall trees. According to the compass, it was not the right one. Nor was the second tall tree. The third one was almost two hundred feet tall.

The pirates began to run towards that tree. Silver hopped after them as fast as he could. He pulled me after him on the rope. I could hear his heavy breathing and his curses when the flies settled on his hot face. From time to time, he gave me a look which filled me with fear. It was clear that he was thinking only of the gold. When he had that, he would kill me and my friends. Then he would sail away.

The pirates were near the hiding-place of the treasure. "Come on, mates!" shouted George Merry. "All together!"

Ten yards from the tree, they all stopped suddenly. Silver and I reached them. We stopped too. In front of us, was a deep hole in the ground. The sides had fallen in. Grass was growing in it. A broken axe and some boards were nearby. On one of the boards was the word, Walrus. That was the name of Flint's ship.

At once, the truth was clear to all of us. The hiding-place had been found sometime ago. The treasure had been taken away. The seven hundred thousand pounds had simply disappeared.

# 32

# SAFE IN BEN GUNN'S CAVE

This was a horrible shock for the pirates. They looked as if they had been struck. Silver alone was calm. He kept his head. Quickly he changed his plan. He handed me a pistol, whispering, "Take that, and be ready for trouble." Then he moved round so that the hole was between us and the five pirates. He freed me from the rope.

Cursing and shouting, the five pirates jumped into the hole. They began to dig with their fingers. Morgan found a piece of gold. He held it up for all to see and he shouted to Silver, "That's your seven hundred thousand pounds, is it?"

"He's fooled us again!" shouted George Merry.

The five of them climbed out of the hole, shouting and cursing. There they stood, the five of them on one side of the hole. Silver and I stood facing them on the other side. "This is the end," I thought. Silver stood there, calm and smiling. He was brave, and no mistake!

George Merry took the lead. "Look at them, lads!" he shouted. "There's the old devil who has been fooling us all the time. And there's that boy who has brought us bad luck. Now, lads!........" He raised his gun to fire at us.

"Crack! Crack! Crack!" Three shots rang out from the trees. Merry fell head-first into the hole. He was dead. Another fell dead on the edge of the hole. Then the other three ran away as fast as they could.

Dr. Livesey, Gray, and Ben Gunn ran out from the trees with guns.

"After them!" shouted the doctor. "Don't let them get the boats!"

We ran fast through the trees and bushes. Silver could not run as fast as we did although he tried hard. After a time, he called to us, "Doctor! look over there. There's no need to hurry."

It was true. We were now between the three pirates and their boats. There was no need for us to hurry. We sat down, breathless. Long John came up to us, hot and tired out. He wiped his face and said, "Thank you, doctor. You came just in time." His eyes fell on Ben Gunn. ``Well!'' he exclaimed, "and so it's you, Ben Gunn, is it?"

"Yes, I'm Ben Gunn, I am. How are you, Mr. Silver? Pretty well, I think."

"Ben! Ben!" Silver said to him, softly, "To think that you've tricked me!"

Slowly we made our way towards the two boats. On the way, the doctor told me what had happened. Ben Gunn had found the treasure some months ago. He had carried it, little by little, to his cave on the hill with two peaks. After the doctor had learned that from Ben Gunn, he had given the map to Silver for it was now quite useless. The doctor and his friends had left the stockade to live with Ben Gunn in his cave. There was plenty of salted goat's meat there, fresh water and wild fruits.

That morning, the doctor had learnt that the pirates were going after the treasure. He, with Ben Gunn and Gray, had run to save me. Ben Gunn had run on ahead for he could run the fastest. It

was his high, shaking voice that had terrified the pirates.

"It was lucky for me that Hawkins was there. You'd never have thought of saving Long John, would you?" Silver asked.

"Never," answered the doctor cheerfully.

By this time, we had reached the boats. The doctor broke one of them to pieces with an axe. We all got into the other and rowed to North Bay. Silver was tired out but he rowed as hard as the rest of us.

When we passed the hill with the two peaks, we saw the mouth of Ben Gunn's cave. Mr. Trelawney was standing there. We waved and gave a loud cheer. Silver joined in the cheering.

Three miles farther on, just inside North Bay, we met the Hispaniola, sailing by herself. The high tide had carried her away from the beach. We anchored her safely. Leaving Gray on guard, we left the ship and rowed back to Ben Gunn's cave.

Mr. Trelawney greeted me very kindly. To Long John, he said, "John Silver, you are an evil fellow. You ought to be hanged. My friends have asked me to let you go free. I shall do so. But those dead men will follow you wherever you go. Be sure of that!"

"Thank you, sir," replied Long John.

"How dare you thank me!" cried the Squire. "Get inside!"

We all went inside the cave. It was large and airy, with a spring of water in one corner. Captain Smollett was lying there. Behind him was a mountain of gold. A mountain of gold bars! It was Flint's treasure—the treasure that had cost so many lives!

"I'm very glad to see you, Jim," Captain Smollett said to me. "You're brave lad, Jim." He saw Silver and asked, "What brings you here, John Silver?"

"I've come back to my duty, sir."

"Ah!" said the captain. That was all he said.

What a supper I had that night, with all my friends round me! We ate Ben Gunn's salted goat's meat. Ben Gunn ate the cheese that we had brought from the Hispaniola. Never was there a happier company. Silver was sitting there too, eating heartily. He joined in our laughter. He was the same pleasant companion that he had been when we first set out.

# 33

# WE SAIL HOME

The next morning we got up very early. There was a lot of work to be done. All that mountain of gold had to be put on board the Hispaniola. There were still three pirates on the island. One of us had to keep watch all the time.

The gold had to be carried about a mile to the beach. Then it was carried by boat to the Hispaniola, which lay about three miles from the shore. It was heavy work. Gray and Ben Gunn did the rowing. Dr. Livesey, Mr. Trelawney and Long John did the carrying. My job was to pack the money into bags. There were all sorts of coins: English, French, Spanish and Portuguese. Day after day, the work went on. My fingers ached. My back ached. I

was sick of the sight of gold!

All this time, we had seen nothing of the three pirates. Then, one evening, we heard shouting and singing far off.

"It's the pirates," said the doctor. "All drunk, sir," Silver told him.

We decided to leave them on the island. But we left plenty of food for them together with rope, tools, medicines and tobacco.

It was time for us to sail. The treasure was safe on board. We had water and food to last us till the nearest port. This we reached in five days' time.

The harbour seemed a wonderful place after Treasure Island. The little town was gay with lights. There were fruits and vegetables to be bought. All around us were friendly people.

I went on shore with Dr. Livesey and Mr. Trelawney. We met the captain of an English ship and he invited us on board.

He introduced us to his officers. We had a very pleasant time together and did not leave his ship till dawn.

We found Gray in the cabin with Captain Smollett. Ben Gunn was alone on deck. Silver had gone but he had not gone empty-handed either. He had carried off a bag of gold, worth about four hundred pounds. We did not mind. We were pleased to get rid of him.

The captain took on more men. With the help of these, we made a good voyage home. Only five of the original crew were sailing home. "Drink and the devil had done for the rest!"

All of us had a fair share of the treasure. Some of us used the money wisely, some, foolishly. I gave my share to my mother. She put it at once in the bank for "a rainy day". Captain Smollett retired from the sea. Gray bought a ship. He is married now and the father of a family. Ben Gunn got more than his thousand pounds. He spent it, or lost it, in nineteen days. Then he had to beg for bread. But the Squire found him work as a gardener. Benn is a great favourite in his village. He is quite famous for his singing in church on Sundays.

We never heard anything more of Long John Silver. I suppose he joined his wife and is now living, in comfort, with her and with his parrot.

There is still a treasure of silver bars on Treasure Island, but I will never go back for it. Treasure Island, and Silver's parrot. "Ay! Ay! Sir. Ship ahoy! Seaward ho!"

## CHAPTER 1

*QUESTIONS*

1. Describe the captain's arrival at the Admiral Benbow Inn.

2. How did the captain spend his evenings?

3. Whom was the captain afraid of ?

LANGUAGE PRACTICE

A. *Look at this sentence* :

Although they were afraid of the seaman, they liked the excitement of the stories.

This means :

They were afraid of the seaman. But they liked the excitement of the stories.

*From each pair of sentences below, make one sentence, following the pattern with although :*

1. It is raining. But I shall go out.

2. I am tired. But I must finish my homework.

3. I don't like vegetables. But I eat them.

B. *Look at this sentence* : Call me "captain", that will do.

This means : Call me "captain", that will *be enough.*

In the sentences below, use do in place of be enough :

1. Three yards of silk will be enough for her dress.

2. The meat will be enough for dinner.

3. Will one bottle of milk be enough?

C. *Look at this sentence* : He used to stand on a high rock.

This means : He often stood on a high rock.

*Change each sentence below to the form with used to :*

1. Father often played football when he was a boy.

2. Grandfather often rode a horse when he was young.

3. We often went swimming when we lived near the beach.

## CHAPTER 2

*QUESTIONS*

1. Describe the appearance of Black Dog.

2. What made Jim feel "a sudden pity" for the captain?

3. How did Dr. Livesey help the captain?

LANGUAGE PRACTICE

A. Notice the "*question tags*" in these sentences :

1. You haven't forgotten your old shipmate, have you?

2. We will have a little talk, won't we?

Complete each sentence below with the correct "question tag".

1. You have finished your homework ,.............................. ?

2. They will go by bus, ......................................?

3. Mr. Brown smokes, ......................................?

4. She didn't find her watch, ..............................?

B. *Look at this sentence* : He was a yellow-faced man.

This means : He was a man with a yellow face.

Put the sentences below into the first form :

1. The captain was afraid of the seaman with one leg.

2. Round his head was a bandage with a blood-stain.

3. Mrs. Smith is a woman with a kind heart.

C. Notice the Past Continuous Tense of the Passive Voice in this sentence :

The chairs and the table were being knocked over.

Complete each sentence below with the Past Continuous Tense, Passive Voice of the verb in the brackets :-

1. The match .......................................... in the rain. (play)

2. The meat ........................... while we were waiting. (cook)

3. The money ................. while Mr. Lee was waiting. (count)

## CHAPTER 3

*QUESTIONS*

1. What did the captain tell Jim?

2. What happened in the afternoon of the funeral?

3. What message did Blind Pew bring?

LANGUAGE PRACTICE

A. *Look at this sentence* : I've got to get away from here quickly.

This means: I have to get away from here quickly.

Rewrite each sentence below in the first form :

1. I have to go home at once.

2. We have to wear our summer uniforms.

3. The captain has to stop drinking rum.

B. *Look at this sentence* : It was so evil that I felt frightened.

The second part of the sentence is the Result of the first part. It is an Adverb Clause of Result.

List A contains the first part of the sentence. List B contains the second part. For each sentence, find the correct second part :

| A | B |
| --- | --- |
| 1. The tea was so hot | that we couldn't eat it. |
| 2. The meat was so tough | that we couldn't drink it. |

3.  The night was so dark                      that we fetched the doctor.

4.  Mother was so ill                          that we couldn't see that way.

## CHAPTER 4

### QUESTIONS

1.  What was the Black Spot?

2.  What did Jim find inside the sea-chest?

3.  What did Jim and his mother take from the chest?

### LANGUAGE PRACTICE

A.  *Look at this sentence* :

It belongs to you, Jim, my poor, fatherless boy.

*Fatherless* means, *without a father*.

Find one word to replace the phrase in italics in each of the following sentences :

1.  The child is *without a home*.

2.  Jack is *without help*.

3.  July was a month *without rain*.

B.  *Look at this sentence* :

We caught the sound of *running* feet.

Notice the use of the Present Participle as an Adjective.

Fill in the blanks in these sentences with an Adjective formed from the Present Participle of the verb in the brackets :

1.  She held the ..................... child in her arms. (sleep)

2.  The ..................... man asked for water. (die)

3.  The firemen rushed to the ..................... house. (burn)

## CHAPTER 5

### QUESTIONS

1.  What did Jim see from his hiding-place?

2.  Why was Blind Pew angry?

3.  Describe the end of Blind Pew.

## CHAPTER 6

### QUESTIONS

1.  Say what you know about Mr. Trelawney.

2.  What was inside the book?

3.  What did the map show?

## CHAPTER 7

### QUESTIONS

1.  What did the Squire write in his letter?

2.  What made Jim stop in his reading of the letter?

3.  Why did Jim feel that he was "the luckiest boy in the world"?

LANGUAGE PRACTICE

A.  *Look at the sentence* :

The very next day, the Squire went to Bristol.

Very is used to make the following word stronger.

Make the words in italics in these sentences stronger by putting very in front of them :

1.  At that *moment*, the captain fell down dead.

2.  He is the *man* for the job.

3.  They worked in the *same* office.

B.  Look at this sentence : Never have I felt better.

That means : I have never felt better.

The first form makes the meaning stronger.

Make each sentence below stronger by putting it into the first form :-

1.  I have never seen such a fine palace.

2.  We had never been so hungry.

3.  He has never eaten so much.

## CHAPTER 8

*QUESTIONS*

1.  Describe Long John Silver.

2.  What happened in the Spy-glass Inn?

3.  What did the Squire and Dr. Livesey think about Silver?

LANGUAGE PRACTICE

*Look at these sentences* :

1.  In twenty hours' time, we should be sailing to Treasure Island.

2.  It's about a ten minutes' walk.

Complete each sentence below with the correct phrase from the list:

a two hours' drive            an hour's lesson

a month's voyage            a week's work

1.  From Hong Kong to London by ship is ................................

2.  From here to the next town is ...............................................

3.  After ........................................................ , we have a break.

4.  Cleaning the house is .........................................................

## CHAPTER 9

*QUESTIONS*

1.  Why was Captain Smollett angry?

2.  What two things should be done before the ship sailed?

3.  Why did Jim stay on deck all that night ?

LANGUAGE PRACTICE

*Study this sentence carefully* :

Hardly had we got down to the cabin when a sailor knocked at the door.

This means :

Very soon after we had got down to the cabin, a sailor knocked at the door.

Rewrite each sentence below in the first form beginning with hardly :

1.  Very soon after I had got home, the door-ball rang.

2.  Very soon after we had got to school, the rain began.

3.  Very soon after we had sat down, dinner was brought in.

## CHAPTER 10

*QUESTIONS*

1.  Why was nobody sorry when Mr. Arrow disappeared?

2.  What did his companions think of Long John ?

3.  What do you know about Silver's parrot ?

LANGUAGE PRACTICE

*Look at these sentences* :

(a)  There I would sit for hours.

(b)  There I used to sit for hours.

(c)  There I often sat for hours.

The meaning of each sentence is the same.

Write each sentence below in the (a) and (b) form : (Six sentences altogether)

1.  There Mr. White often stayed for his holidays.

2.  They often rowed to the next island.

3.  Sailors often went to the Inn for rum.

## CHAPTER 11

*QUESTIONS*

1.  What was Silver's plan?

2.  Why was Jim "too frightened to move"?

3.  Did the pirates find Jim in the apple barrel?

LANGUAGE PRACTICE

*Look at this sentence* :

I was in charge of the stores because of my leg.

This means :

I was in charge of the stores because I had only one leg.

Rewrite each sentence below in the first form :

1.  We stayed at home because the weather was bad.

2.  I can't play because I must do my homework.

3.  They couldn't come because they had an accident.

## CHAPTER 12

*QUESTIONS*

1. Why was Silver disappointed?
2. What were Captain Smollett's three points?
3. Who were the loyal men on the ship?

### LANGUAGE PRACTICE

*Notice the Passive Infinitive in this sentence:*

I've ordered rum to be served out to all of you.

Fill in each blank in the sentences below with the Passive Infinitive of the verb in the brackets:

1. You ought .........(hang)
2. The gold had ...........to the ship. (carry)
3. There was fruit ..........(buy)

## CHAPTER 13

*QUESTIONS*

1. What made Jim hate the island from the start?
2. Why did Captain Smollett send the men ashore?
3. What did Jim do?

### LANGUAGE PRACTICE

*Look at this sentence:*

At any moment the mutiny *might* begin.

*Might* is the Past of *may*. Here *might* means could *with a sense of doubt.*

*Rewrite these sentences, using might in the place of could:*

1. The boy could lose his way in the wood.
2. We thought we could have a holiday.
3. The pirates could kill Jim.

## CHAPTER 14

*QUESTIONS*

1. What happened to Tom?
2. What made Jim ran as he had never run before?
3. Why were Jim's thoughts "desperate ones"?

### LANGUAGE PRACTICE

*Notice the use of the Perfect Infinitive in this sentence :*

That would have been the end of Jim Hawkins.

The Perfect Infinitive is used for an action in the Past.

Fill in the blanks in these sentences with the Perfect Infinitive of the verb in the brackets :

1. Mr. Chan ought to .........................last night. (arrive)
2. I should .........................yesterday if I had been well. (come)
3. You should .................to the doctor when you first felt ill. (go)

## CHAPTER 15

*QUESTIONS*

1. What did Ben Gunn look like?
2. Tell Ben Gunn's story.
3. How could Jim get back to the Hispaniola?

LANGUAGE PRACTICE

Look at this sentence : Three years, *all by myself.*

This means : Three years, *all alone.*

*Rewrite each sentence below in the first form*:

1. Since his wife's death, Mr. Wong has lived all alone.
2. They stayed on the beach, all alone.
3. We were all alone in the forest.

## CHAPTER 16

*QUESTIONS*

1. Describe the stockade.
2. Why could the six pirates not stop the loading of the boat?
3. Who went to the stockade with the doctor?

LANGUAGE PRACTICE

A. *Look at this sentence*:

If there had been a wind, we should have attacked the pirates.

This is a Conditional Sentence where the action refers to the Past.

Fill in each blank with the right tense of the verb in the brackets:

1. Last Sunday, if the weather had been fine, we .............. (go out)
2. If you .................:. to bed early last night, you would have felt fresh this morning. (go)
3. He .............his last examination if he had worked harder. (pass)

B. *Look at this sentence* :

A wide space had been cleared.

The tense is the Past Perfect in the Passive Voice.

This sentence, in the Active Voice is :

Somebody had cleared a wide space.

Rewrite each sentence below using the Passive Voice:

1. Somebody had found the treasure.
2. Somebody had carried the gold off.
3. Somebody had told the headmaster.

## CHAPTER 17

*QUESTIONS*

1. What made the trip to the stockade so dangerous?
2. What caused the boat to sink?
3. What harm was done by the sinking of the boat?

## LANGUAGE PRACTICE

A. *Look at this sentence* :

We rushed there in order to arrive there first.

This means:

We rushed there so that we could arrive there first.

*Rewrite these sentences in the first form, with in order to* :

1. I got up early so that I could finish my homework.

2. He went to London so that he could see the Queen.

3. Jim ran so that he might escape.

B. *Look at this sentence*:

The water seemed likely to sink the boat.

*This means*:

The water seemed as if it must sink the boat.

*Rewrite these sentences in the first form with likely* :

1. The branch seemed as if it must break.

2. The ship seemed as if it must sink.

3. It seemed as if it must rain.

## CHAPTER 18

### QUESTIONS

1. What was the "first success" of the doctor and his party?

2. What had Captain Smollett carried away from the Hispaniola?

3. What did Captain Smollett write in his log-book?

## LANGUAGE PRACTICE

*Look at this sentence* :

No damage *at all* was done.

*At all* makes the Negative stronger.

Make these sentences stronger by using at all :

1. He gave no answer...................................................................

2. She eats no bread.................................................................

3. We bought nothing ...............................................................

## CHAPTER 19

### QUESTIONS

1. What made the log-house a sad and uncomfortable place?

2. Why did the doctor tell Jim, "there's hope for us yet"?

3. What awakened Jim?

## CHAPTER 20

### QUESTIONS

1. What offer did Silver make to Captain Smollett?

2. What was Captain Smollett's offer to Silver?

3. Why did Captain Smollett say that the pirates were "in a nasty corner"?

## LANGUAGE PRACTICE

A. *Look at this sentence* :

You had better sit down.

This means :

It is better for you to sit down.

Rewrite these sentences in the first form, *with had better* :

1. It is better for you to take your umbrella.

2. It is better for us to hurry.

3. It is better for them to be quiet.

B. *Look at this sentence* :

If you would rather, you can stay here.

The meaning of would rather is prefer or like more.

Rewrite these sentences in the first form, with would rather :

1. Write, or read if you prefer.

2. Draw a house, or a tree if you prefer.

3. Go with him, or come with us if you prefer.

## CHAPTER 21

*QUESTIONS*

1. What orders did Captain Smollett give to the party?

2. What was the "heavy price" that they had paid for their victory?

3. What made Captain Smollett say, "We'll beat them yet?

## LANGUAGE PRACTICE

*Look at this sentence* :

Now, of the four pirates, only one was unwounded.

Unwounded means not wounded.

Similarly make one word of the two words in italics in each sentence below :

1. The island was *not inhabited*.

2. The log-house was *not damaged*.

3. There he stood, *not decided* what to do next.

## CHAPTER 22

*QUESTIONS*

1. What was Jim's plan?

2. What do you know about Ben Gunn's boat?

3. What did Jim see through the cabin window?

**LANGUAGE PRACTICE**

A.  *Look at this sentence* :

I would *prevent* them *from doing* that.

Complete these sentences, using from and the correct form of the verb in the brackets :

1.  A bad cold prevented me .......................... to school. (come)

2.  Her cough prevented her ...................................... (speak)

3.  A fierce dog prevented Tom ........................ the gate. (enter)

B.  Look at this sentence :

In spite of the danger, I fell asleep.

This means :

Although I was in danger, I fell asleep

*Rewrite these sentences in the first form with in spite of* :

1.  Although I was hungry, I could not eat.

2.  Although it was hot, he was wearing a coat.

3.  Although he was wounded, he moved fast.

## CHAPTER 23

**QUESTIONS**

1.  Where was Jim when he woke up?

2.  What made Jim forget his thirst?

3.  For what reasons did Jim decide to go on board?

## CHAPTER 24

**QUESTIONS**

1.  Whom did Jim find on the deck of the Hispaniola?

2.  What was the bargain that Jim made with Hands?

3.  Why was Jim feeling very pleased with himself ?

**LANGUAGE PRACTICE**

*Look at this sentence*:

I've come on board to take charge of the ship.

The meaning is :

I've come on board to look after the ship.

Rewrite these sentences, with take charge of in place of look after:

1.  The head clerk will look after the office while the manager is away.

2.  Who will look after the children if their mother dies?

3.  Miss Ho looked after our class when Miss Wong was ill.

## CHAPTER 25

**QUESTIONS**

1.  Why did Hands ask Jim to go below for some wine?

2.  What happened when the Hispaniola struck the beach?

3. What caused the death of Israel hands?

**CHAPTER 26**

*QUESTIONS*

1. What made Jim feel "sick and faint"?
2. Why did he feel suddenly afraid?
3. What awakened the pirates?

**LANGUAGE PRACTICE**

A. *Look at this sentence* : I did not mind that.

This means:

I did not worry about that.

*Rewrite these sentences in the first form with mind instead of worry about*:

1. Don't worry about her!
2. Dead or alive, who worries about Ben Gunn?
3. I don't worry about what you say.

B. *Notice the Present Continuous Infinitive, Active Voice in this sentence* :

It was time for me *to be going*.

*Complete these sentences, using the Present Continous Infinitive of the verb in the brackets*:

1. It was too early for us ........................................ (get up)
2. He is too young ........................................ a car. (drive)
3. Will you ...................... that letter this evening? (write)
4. A dead man should not ......................... like that. (lie)

**CHAPTER 27**

*QUESTIONS*

1. Whom did Jim find in the stockade?
2. What did Silver tell Jim?
3. What bargain did Silver make with Jim?

**CHAPTER 28**

*QUESTIONS*

1. What did Jim see through the loop-hole?
2. What complaints did George Merry make?
3. How did Silver win the pirates to his side?

**LANGUAGE PRACTICE**

Notice the use of the Gerund after the preposition in this sentence : You're thinking of being captain.

Fill in each blank with the gerund of the verb in the brackets:

1. He is thinking of .................................... to London. (fly)
2. He spoke about ........................................ tomorrow. (leave)
3. He was punished for ............................. the rules. (break)

## CHAPTER 29

QUESTIONS

1. Why did Jim feel ashamed?
2. What advice did the doctor give to Silver?
3. What puzzled Silver?

LANGUAGE PRACTICE

*Look at these sentences* :

1. He worked as if he were visiting an English family.
2. The men behaved as if he were still the ship's doctor.

Notice the use of were in place of was after as if .......

Fill in the blanks in these sentences with the right form of the verb to be :

1. George Merry spoke as if he .......................... the captain.
2. I walked as if I ...................................... drunk.
3. She screamed as if she ...................................... mad.

## CHAPTER 30

QUESTIONS

1. Why were the pirates in better spirits?
2. What puzzled the pirates?
3. What was Flint's pointer?

LANGUAGE PRACTICE

A. *Look at this sentence* : My spirits were low.

The meaning is : I was sad and troubled.

The opposite is : My spirits were high. This means: I was very cheerful.

*Rewrite the sentences below in the first form* :

1. He was troubled after hearing the bad news.
2. They were very cheerful after their dinner.
3. Jim was sad after his father's funeral.

B. Look at this sentence :  It makes me cold inside to think of Flint.

That sentence may also be written thus: To think of Flint makes me cold inside.

*Rewrite the sentences below in the first form, beginning with it* :

1. To cut a Bible brings bad luck.
2. To dig a field is hard work.
3. To learn English takes a long time.

## CHAPTER 31

QUESTIONS

1. What terrified the pirates?
2. What made the pirates cheerful again?
3. What did the pirates find when they reached the hiding-place of the treasure?

**LANGUAGE PRACTICE**

A.  *Look at this sentence* :

Then he moved round so that the hole was between us and the pirates.

The second part of the sentence gives the Purpose of the first part. It is an Adverb Clause of Purpose.

List A contains the first part of the sentence. List B contains the second part.

Find the right ending for each beginning :

|           A            |             B              |
| She drinks milk        | so that I might catch the bus. |
| He got up early        | so that she may keep well. |
| They ate a lot         | so that he finished his homework. |
| I ran fast             | so that they grew fat. |

B.  Look at this sentence :   He was brave, and *no mistake*.

This means :         He was certainly brave.

*Rewrite these sentences in the first form with and no mistake at the end*:

1.  We were certainly hungry.

2.  The bus is certainly late.

3.  The weather is certainly hot.

## CHAPTER 32

*QUESTIONS*

1.  What made Jim think, "This is the end"?

2.  How were Jim and Silver saved from the pirates?

3.  What did Mr. Livesey tell Jim?

4.  What did Jim see inside Ben Gunn's cave?

## CHAPTER 33

*QUESTIONS*

1.  How was the treasure taken to the Hispaniola?

2.  What happened to   (a) the three pirates?

                       (b) Long John Silver?

What did Jim and his friends do with their share of the treasure?

**LANGUAGE PRACTICE**

*Look at these sentences*:

1.  Gray and Ben Gunn did the rowing.

2.  Dr. Livesey, Mr. Trelawney and Long John did the carrying.

Notice the use of the Gerund.

Complete each sentence below with a gerund formed from the verb in the brackets :

1.  I did the ...................................... (pack)

2. We saw the ......................................(fight)

3. The ................. and the ................ were far off. (shout, sing)

B. Look at the sentence :   We were pleased to get rid of him.

    The meaning is :       We were pleased to throw him off.

Rewrite these sentences in the first form, using to get rid of:

1. I can't throw off my cold.

2. You must throw off your laziness!

3. The pirates wanted to throw off Long John Silver.

# GREAT STORIES IN EASY ENGLISH